前言

出國旅遊很愉快，但是英文該怎麼辦？

世界很大，想去的地方也很多，像是紐約、倫敦、巴黎、澳洲，數都數不完。但是，即使愉快的國外旅行就在眼前，卻也有許多人因為英文而感到壓力——入境審查、購物、點餐等，光是想到必須使用英文的情況，就全身直冒冷汗。而就算是參加有導遊的旅行團，會說一兩句英文與完全不懂英文，還是有很大的差異。本書是為了擔心英文而對出國旅遊猶豫不決的人、為了就算只有一句也想多懂一點英文的人、為了讓出國旅遊更自由的人、為了出發旅行前想先學點英語的人而寫成的。

只要替換句型中的單字，就能說好英文！

本書不是讓你單純帶著上路，在必要時翻找適當語句的句型書，而是讓你在**出發旅行之前，可以先學點東西的書**。因此，全書並不是以狀況為主列出必需句型，而是以句型為學習重心的架構寫成。**簡單來說，句型就是公式**。只要替換句型中的單字，就可以說出各種句子，即便是不懂英文的初級學習者，也能有效熟悉句子。本書整理了旅途中必備的 50 個句型，這些句型可以在各種情境中，如飛機餐、入境審查、點餐時派上用場。

現在開始有自信地出國旅行吧！

旅行是一連串的新挑戰。出國旅遊時，那怕只有一句，也請試著開口活用學過的句型吧！外國人聽懂自己說的話時的喜悅、得到想要的東西時的快樂，都會成為不亞於旅行本身的歡樂和令人難忘的禮物。只要透過本書細細學習，即使是不懂英文的人也可以帶著自信出國旅遊！我們希望通過本書，使更多人能更輕鬆愉快地出國旅遊。

為各位的國外旅遊加油！

裴鎮英・姜旼正

本書特點

為中高齡讀者量身打造

本書將字體放大，讓視力不好的人讀起來也很舒服，而透過玲瓏可愛的插畫與照片，眼睛也能愉快地學習。另外，本書附有音標發音單元，並為每個單字標上音標，所以就算是不熟悉的英文字也能輕鬆地讀出。

利用 50 個句型輕鬆熟悉各種語句

本書從享用飛機餐、搭公車、入住飯店等時刻，或在旅遊地點經常遇上的狀況中，挑選出最常用的語句，並以句型連結，只要更換句型中的單字就可以和人溝通，不懂英文的人也能輕鬆地學起來。出發旅行前，只要學好本書列出的 50 個必備句型就很夠用了。

提供有用的旅遊資訊

本書也特別針對想到國外旅遊就茫然害怕的讀者，提供一系列從填寫入境卡開始，到讀各種標誌的方法等，各式各樣與旅行相關的有用小技巧。在書中各處都藏著微小的資訊，讀著讀著就再也不會對國外旅遊感到害怕了。

音檔光碟、QR 碼、迷你書等豐富的附加資料

本書為自學的讀者，免費提供課文、例句、單字的音檔光碟，也可隨時利用智慧型手機掃描 QR 碼聽音檔、學發音，非常方便。另外，也提供整理出旅行時必備的英文語句及單字的迷你書，尺寸小又輕巧，旅行時隨身攜帶也不成負擔。

本書構成

第一部分　提前了解

在正式進入課本單元之前，書中還整理出到國外旅遊前最好先了解的事項。在**〈準備國外旅遊的 Q&A〉**中，以問答的形式整理出在踏上令人悸動的旅程之前，必須要準備的事情。而在**〈原來很簡單的出國手續〉**中，則以圖標表示，整理出機場的利用方法，不論是誰都能輕易理解。

第二部分　正課學習

本書把在國外旅遊時，一定會碰上的狀況分為 9 大主題、25 個單元，每一單元都有 2 個、全書共 50 個**必備句型**要學習。在每單元中的**〈句型練習〉**部分，都可以讓你將各種單字帶入句型，練習開口說。而在各單元中的**〈對話〉**部分，則可以確認前面學的句型，在實際對話中該如何運用。各個單元的最後，可以在**〈驗收〉**的部分再次挑戰、練習，並整理學過的內容。在每個主題最後的**〈尋找英文吧！〉**中，可以熟悉各種英文標誌的意義，**〈生動的旅遊情報〉**則可以獲得與旅行相關的其他各種資訊。

第三部分　認識更多

這是為了加深學到的句型而製作的額外環節。將**〈句型練習〉**中的所有句子整理，以複習前面學過的句型及造句，並收錄中英文音檔，只要用聽的就能自然而然地學習。另外在**〈美式英語 vs. 英式英語〉**中，則列舉了美國與英國對同一物品的不同用字習慣。

第四部分　旅行英語迷你書

為了在旅行時也能隨時學習、實際應用，這本迷你書中整理出旅行的必需語句及必備單字。因為是一手就能掌握的輕巧尺寸，也很適合隨身攜帶。

目錄

第一部分 **提前了解**

準備國外旅遊的 Q&A · 14
原來很簡單的出國手續 · 16
原來很簡單的海外入境手續 · 18
音標發音表 · 20

第二部分 **正課學習**

在飛機上

1 飛機餐 · 26
句型 01 請問你要喝點什麼嗎？
句型 02 （請給我）牛肉，謝謝。

2 機內服務 · 32
句型 03 可以給我一條毯子嗎？
句型 04 能請你收走我的托盤嗎？

入境時

3 入境審查 · 42
句型 05 我來這裡觀光。
句型 06 我計畫待十天。

4 領取行李 · 48
句型 07 你的航班號碼是什麼（幾號）？
句型 08 你有行李託運存根嗎？

5 公車 · 58
句型 09 哪班公車會到時代廣場？
句型 10 這班公車會到時代廣場嗎？

6 計程車 · 64
句型 11 可以請你帶我去 Sun 飯店嗎？
句型 12 到飯店要花多久時間？

7 地下鐵 · 70
句型 13 你知道售票處在哪裡嗎？
句型 14 我需要一張一日票。

8 入住飯店 · 80
句型 15 我想要辦理入住。
句型 16 我想要一間有一張單人床的房間。

9 使用飯店設施、服務 · 86
句型 17 餐廳在哪裡？
句型 18 有客房服務嗎？

10 解決飯店的問題 · 92
句型 19 空調故障了。
句型 20 沒有衛生紙。

11 飯店退房 · 98
句型 21 對於這個錯誤，我很抱歉。
句型 22 可以用信用卡結帳嗎？

在餐廳

12 預訂餐廳・108
句型 23 我想預訂今天晚上的位子。
句型 24 我們可以坐窗邊的座位嗎？

13 點餐・114
句型 25 這個有附沙拉嗎？
句型 26 你推薦什麼作為主餐？

14 對餐廳的不滿之處・120
句型 27 這個太鹹了。
句型 28 我沒有點沙拉。

15 速食餐廳・126
句型 29 我要一個起司漢堡。
句型 30 不要冰塊，謝謝。

16 咖啡廳・132
句型 31 我要一杯拿鐵。
句型 32 你可以給我一個杯套嗎？

購物時

17 買衣服・144
句型 33 我正在找一件夾克。
句型 34 （你們）這個有更大的尺寸嗎？

18 殺價・150
句型 35 這隻手錶多少錢？
句型 36 這些手錶在特價嗎？

19 換貨與退貨・156
句型 37 我可以把這個換成更大的尺寸嗎？
句型 38 我想退這件裙子。

20 旅遊諮詢處 · 166
句型 39 你可以推薦有趣的博物館嗎？
句型 40 有（任何）遊覽行程嗎？

21 劇院 · 172
句型 41 (請給我)一張《貓》的票，謝謝。
句型 42 表演幾點開始？

22 博物館 · 178
句型 43 今天博物館幾點關閉？
句型 44 我可以在哪裡拿到博物館地圖？

23 找路 · 188
句型 45 我要怎麼去中央公園？
句型 46 最近的公車站牌在哪裡？

24 失竊報案 · 194
句型 47 這附近有警察局嗎？
句型 48 我的包包被偷了。

25 登機手續 · 204
句型 49 我可以看看你的護照嗎？
句型 50 我可以坐靠窗的座位嗎？

認識更多

讓旅行變簡單的句型造句練習 · 228
互有不同的美式英語 vs. 英式英語 · 254

旅行英語迷你書

讓旅行變簡單的旅行英語迷你書

旅行英語 句型搶先看

句型 01 **Would you like** something to drink? 請問你要喝點什麼嗎？

句型 02 Beef, **please**. （請給我）牛肉，謝謝。

句型 03 **Can I get** a blanket? 可以給我一條毯子嗎？

句型 04 **Could you** take my tray? 能請你收走我的托盤嗎？

句型 05 **I'm here** for sightseeing. 我來這裡觀光。

句型 06 **I plan to stay for** ten days. 我計畫待十天。

句型 07 **What's your** flight number? 你的航班號碼是什麼（幾號）？

句型 08 **Do you have** your baggage claim ticket? 你有行李託運存根嗎？

句型 09 **Which bus goes to** Times Square? 哪班公車會到時代廣場？

句型 10 **Does this bus go to** Times Square? 這班公車會到時代廣場嗎？

句型 11 **Could you take me to** the Sun Hotel? 可以請你帶我去 Sun 飯店嗎？

句型 12 **How long does it take to get to** the hotel? 到飯店要花多久時間？

句型 13 **Do you know where** the ticket office **is**? 你知道售票處在哪裡嗎？

句型 14 **I need** a one-day pass. 我需要一張一日票。

句型 15 **I'd like to** check in. 我想要辦理入住。

句型 16 **I'd like a room with** a single bed. 我想要一間有一張單人床的房間。

句型 17 **Where is** the restaurant? 餐廳在哪裡？

句型 18 **Is there** room service? 有客房服務嗎？

句型 19 The air conditioner **doesn't work**. 空調故障了。

句型 20 **There is no** toilet paper. 沒有衛生紙。

句型 21 **I'm sorry for** the error. 對於這個錯誤，我很抱歉。

句型 22 **Is it possible to** pay by credit card? 可以用信用卡結帳嗎？

句型 23 **I'd like to book a table for** tonight. 我想預訂今天晚上的位子。

句型 24 **Could we have a table** by the window? 我們可以坐窗邊的座位嗎？

句型 25 **Does it come with** a salad? 這個有附沙拉嗎？

句型 26 **What do you recommend for** a main dish? 你推薦什麼作為主餐？

句型 27 **This is too** salty. 這個太鹹了。

句型 28 **I didn't order** a salad. 我沒有點沙拉。

句型 29 **I'd like** a cheeseburger. 我要一個起司漢堡。

句型 30 **No** ice, **please**. 不要冰塊，謝謝。

句型 31 **I'll have** a latte. 我要一杯拿鐵。

句型 32 **Can you give me** a sleeve? 你可以給我一個杯套嗎？

句型 33 **I'm looking for** a jacket. 我正在找一件夾克。

句型 34 **Do you have this in** a bigger size? （你們）這個有更大的尺寸嗎？

句型 35 **How much is** this watch? 這隻手錶多少錢？

句型 36 **Are these** watches **on sale**? 這些手錶在特價嗎？

句型 37 **Can I exchange this for** a bigger size? 我可以把這個換成更大的尺寸嗎？

句型 38 **I'd like to get a refund on** this skirt. 我想退這件裙子。

句型 39 **Can you recommend** an interesting museum? 你可以推薦有趣的博物館嗎？

句型 40 **Are there any** tours? 有（任何）遊覽行程嗎？

句型 41 **One ticket for** *Cats*, **please**. （請給我）一張《貓》的票，謝謝。

句型 42 **What time does** the show **start**? 表演幾點開始？

句型 43 **What time does** the museum **close today**? 今天博物館幾點關閉？

句型 44 **Where can I** get a map of the museum? 我可以在哪裡拿到博物館地圖？

句型 45 **How can I get to** Central Park? 我要怎麼去中央公園？

句型 46 **Where is the nearest** bus stop? 最近的公車站牌在哪裡？

句型 47 **Is there a** police station **around here**? 這附近有警察局嗎？

句型 48 **My** bag **was stolen**. 我的包包被偷了。

句型 49 **Can I see your** passport? 我可以看看你的護照嗎？

句型 50 **Can I have** a window seat? 我可以坐靠窗的座位嗎？

第一部分
提前了解

準備國外旅遊 Q&A

Q 護照什麼時候用？

A 國外旅遊時不可或缺的物品就是 passport（護照）。護照在國外會成為自己的身分證明，在搭乘飛機時需要、出入境時需要，連入住飯店也有要求提供身分證件的情況。雖然台灣護照效期多半很長，但出國前最好還是確認一下，護照效期是否還有六個月以上，以免上不了飛機。

Q 去旅行一定需要簽證嗎？

A visa（簽證）是指能入境某國家的許可證。最近如果是以觀光為旅行目的，許多國家允許在一定期間內，不需要簽證也可以入境。以美國來說，如果是觀光旅行的情況，只要事前上網於 ESTA（旅遊許可電子系統）申請許可，就算沒有簽證也能夠待在美國 90 天。不過在入境審查時，必須表明是去觀光，若說去工作或讀書，就有可能遭到拒絕入境。

Q 要怎麼樣才能買到便宜的機票呢？

A 根據購買時機的不同，機票的價格可說是天差地別。想要購買便宜的機票，可以利用各航空公司的促銷活動，或最少在三個月前就先預約。隨著旺季與淡季的不同，價格變動非常大，如果時間上允許的話，旅行時間選在淡季也是不錯的方法。另外，比起直航，要轉機的機票當然比較便宜，不過缺點是很花時間，必須考慮時間、金錢與體力再做選擇。

Q 要在哪裡換錢才好呢？

A 雖然在機場也有可以換匯的 Currency Exchange（換匯所），不過那裡的換匯手續費偏高，因此先在常交易的銀行換錢會比較好。最近利用網路換匯的話，可以得到手續費優惠，因此利用網路換匯也是很好的辦法。

Q 一定要保旅行平安險嗎？

A 雖然保險都只是預防萬一的情況，但有了旅行平安險，若在旅行途中發生事故或遺失物品，多半都能得到直接的補償。就算旅行之前沒辦法提前準備，也可以在機場買保險，不過買保險時，請仔細確認補償的金額和承保範圍。

Q 在國外想用智慧型手機的話該怎麼做？

A 到國外旅行查找地圖或旅遊資訊時，經常會使用智慧型手機，但一不小心可能會產生高額費用。不過，如果事先申請了上網流量，只要繳付一定金額就可以隨心所欲使用漫遊，非常方便。另外，也可申辦隨身機器 Pocket WiFi（口袋 wifi 機），就能自由使用無線網路，或購買能使用一定通話量及上網流量的預付卡等方法。

原來很簡單的出國手續

01

抵達機場

請至少在飛機起飛時間兩小時之前抵達機場。假期或旺季時，最好再留更多時間，於起飛前三小時抵達機場。

02

登機手續

登機手續要到所搭乘的航空公司報到櫃台辦理。查看機場大廳的電子螢幕，可以確認自己的報到櫃台在哪裡。向櫃台出示護照及（電子）機票後，就可以取得登機證並托運行李。

07

等待登機

出境審查結束後，就會進入航站內的管制區。可以在免稅商店購物，或在餐廳、咖啡廳用餐打發時間。

08

登機

飛機登機時間會在實際起飛時間前大約 30 ~ 40 分鐘開始。在登機證上寫有登機時間與登機口，請仔細確認，並準時到達登機口登機。

檢疫申報

若攜帶寵物或植物，在出國前要事先獲得相關單位的證明書，並在海關進行申報。有需要再行申報就可以了。

海關申報

若攜帶貴重物品或高價品，請在出國之前先進行申報。如果沒有申報，回國時被發現可能需要繳付稅金。

出境審查

出示護照並接受出境審查。最近因為有自動通關，事先申請的話就不需要另外接受檢查，可以快速過關。

安全檢查

進到出境管制區後，需要進行安全檢查。讓行李通過 X 光檢查機，檢查是否有尖銳或違禁物品。

原來很簡單的海外入境手續

01

填寫文件

在飛機上，空服員會發放入境卡及海關申報單。如果到了機場才填寫，可能會因為排隊的人變多，而要花更多時間才能入境。在機內提前寫好這些表單的話，可以節省時間。

02

抵達機場

下了飛機後，跟著 Arrival（抵達）的標誌移動就能入境。如果是要轉乘其他飛機，就跟著寫有 Transfer（轉乘）的標誌走。

07

抵達入境大廳

結束所有入境過程後，就可以從 Arrival Hall（入境大廳）出去。如果有前來接機的人，請在這裡與他會合。

08

前往市區

若要移動到市區，請利用 Subway（地下鐵）、Bus（公車）、Taxi（計程車）等交通工具。另外，也可利用 Car Rental（租車）來移動。

等待入境審查

要接受入境審查，需要排隊。請在 Visitors（訪客）、Non-citizen（非公民）或 Foreigner（外國人）區域等候。

入境審查

入境審查官會一對一詢問來訪目的、期程與住宿地點等。不要緊張並誠實地回答就可以了。有的國家，會要求拍攝臉部照片或按壓指紋。

海關申報

通常只要將 Customs Form（海關申報單）交給職員後走出去即可。海關申報單每個家庭只需要填寫一張。有需要再行申報即可。

領取行李

到 Baggage Claim（行李領取處）領取出發時託運的行李。行李會出現在迴轉式輸送帶上，只要等自己的行李出來拿走就可以了。

音標發音表

單母音		
[i]	嘴形呈扁平狀，發出類似「一～」的長音。	read [rid] 閱讀
[ɪ]	嘴形呈扁平狀，發出類似「一」的短促音。	fix [fɪks] 修理
[e]	發音類似「せ一」的長音。	gate [get] 門
[ɛ]	嘴巴呈扁平狀，發音類似「せ」，短促音。	desk [dɛsk] 書桌
[æ]	下巴往下，嘴巴張大，發出類似「せ」的短音。	cat [kæt] 貓
[ɑ]	張大嘴巴，發出類似「Ｙ」音。	box [bɑks] 箱子
[o]	略微張大嘴巴，嘴脣嘟起，發出「ㄡ」的長音。	door [dor] 門
[ɔ]	發音類似「ㄛ」，短促音。	chalk [tʃɔk] 粉筆
[u]	嘴巴呈嘟嘴狀，發出「ㄨ～」的長音。	spoon [spun] 湯匙
[ʊ]	嘴巴呈嘟嘴狀， 發出類出「ㄨ」的短促音。	look [lʊk] 看
[ʌ]	嘴巴呈大橢圓形，發音時肚子內縮，像被打一拳一樣，發出的音介於「Ｙ」和「ㄛ」之間。	cup [kʌp] 杯子
[ə]	嘴巴呈小橢圓形， 發出類似「ㄜ」，但不捲舌。	afraid [ə`fred] 害怕
[ɚ]	稍微張開嘴巴，捲起一半的舌尖，發音類似「ㄦ」，多用在輕音節。	finger [`fɪŋgɚ] 手指
[ɝ]	稍微張開嘴巴，捲起整個舌頭，發音類似「ㄦ」，多用在重音節。	girl [gɝl] 女孩
雙母音		
[aɪ]	先發「Ｙ」，再發短的「一」，兩個音中間不斷開。	tiger [`taɪgɚ] 老虎
[aʊ]	先發「Ｙ」，再發短的「ㄨ」，兩個音中間不斷開。	cow [kaʊ] 乳牛
[ɔɪ]	先發「ㄛ」，再發短的「一」，兩個音中間不斷開。	boy [bɔɪ] 男孩

無聲子音：聲帶不振動，氣音較多		
[p]	緊閉嘴唇，大量吐氣沖開雙唇，發類似「ㄆ」。	pen [pɛn] 筆
[t]	將舌尖緊貼上牙齒，大量吐氣彈開舌尖，發「ㄊ」。	tender [`tɛndɚ] 柔軟的
[k]	將舌根稍微隆起，大量吐氣衝開舌根，發「ㄎ」音。	kite [kaɪt] 風箏
[f]	齒輕碰下唇，吐氣時氣流大量衝開唇齒接觸點，發「ㄈ」。	foot [fʊt] 腳

00-0

[s]	將牙齒合上，舌尖頂住牙齒，吐氣時氣流大量衝過舌齒接觸點，發類似「ㄙ」音。	study [`stʌdɪ] 學習
[θ]	嘴巴微張，舌尖放在上下齒之間，往舌尖大量吐氣，舌頭後縮，發類似「ㄙ」音。	think [θɪŋk] 想
[ʃ]	嘴形呈發出「ㄨ」的樣子，舌頭平放，發類似「ㄒㄩ」音。	ship [ʃip] 船
[tʃ]	舌尖頂住上牙齦，瞬間彈開時發類似「ㄑㄩ」音。	church [tʃɝtʃ] 教會
[h]	吐氣摩擦軟顎的聲音，類似「ㄏ」音。	hot [hɑt] 熱的
有聲子音：聲帶振動，氣音較少，氣流磨擦處振動較大		
[b]	緊閉嘴唇，吐氣衝開雙唇，發類似「ㄅ」音。	bed [bɛd] 床
[d]	將舌尖緊貼上牙齒，吐氣彈開舌尖，發「ㄉ」。	doctor [`dɑktɚ] 醫生
[g]	將舌根稍微隆起，吐氣沖開舌根，發「ㄍ」音。	give [gɪv] 給予
[v]	齒碰觸下唇，吐氣時唇齒不分開，氣流摩擦唇齒接觸點造成較大力的振動，發音類似有聲的「ㄈ」。	very [`vɛrɪ] 非常
[z]	將牙齒合上，舌尖頂住牙齒，吐氣時舌齒不分開，氣流摩擦舌齒接觸點，大力振動，發類似有聲的「ㄙ」音。	zoo [zu] 動物園
[ð]	嘴巴微張，舌尖放在上下齒之間，往舌尖大量吐氣，舌頭後縮，發介於「ㄉㄌ」之間的音。	they [ðe] 他們
[ʒ]	嘴形呈發出「ㄨ」的樣子，舌頭平放，發類似「ㄐㄩ」音。	usual [`juʒʊəl] 通常
[dʒ]	舌尖頂住上牙齦，瞬間彈開時發類似「ㄐㄩ」音。	joy [dʒɔɪ] 歡樂
[m]	（母音前）類似「ㄇ」的音。（母音後）嘴巴閉上，發出鼻音。	match [mætʃ] 火柴
[n]	（母音前）類似「ㄋ」的音。（母音後）嘴巴微張，舌尖頂住上牙齦，發出鼻音。	neighborhood [`nebɚ,hʊd] 鄰近地區
[ŋ]	（只出現在母音後）類似「ㄥ」的鼻音。	sing [sɪŋ] 唱歌
[l]	（母音前）類似「ㄌ」音。（母音後）舌尖頂住上牙齦，發出類似「勒」的音。	lily [`lɪlɪ] 百合花
[r]	舌尖往後捲起，發介於「ㄦ」音。	bread [brɛd] 麵包
[j]	嘴形呈扁平狀，快速地連著發出「ㄧㄜ」的短促音。	yawn [jɔn] 打呵欠
[w]	嘴巴呈嘟嘴狀，快速地連著發出「ㄨㄜ」的短促音。	watch [wɑtʃ] 手錶

第二部分
正課學習

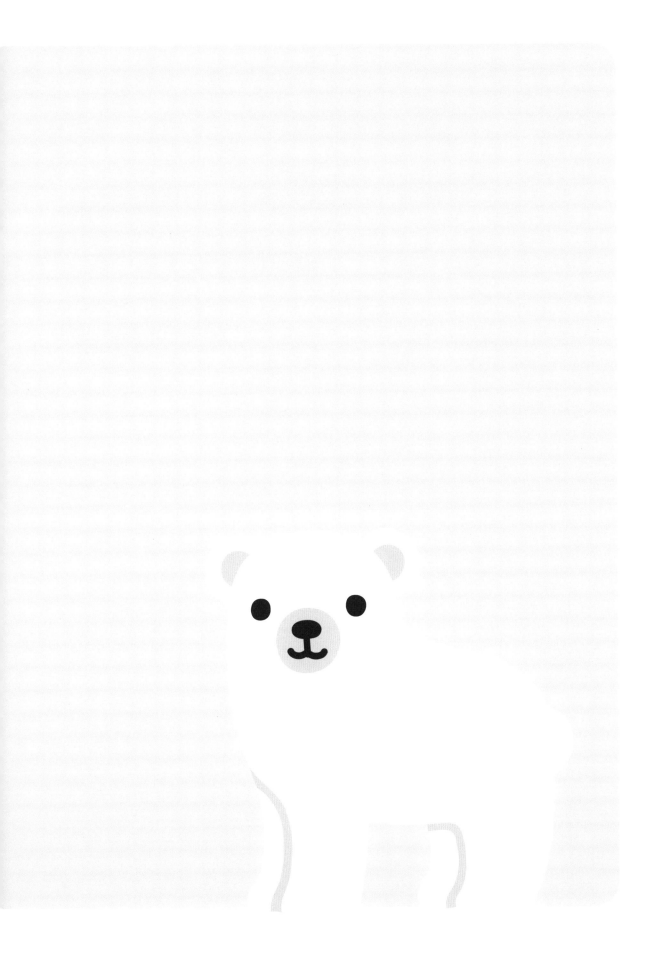

在飛機上

01 飛機餐

02 機內服務

01 飛機餐

請聽以下對話，並跟著說說看。 01-1

對話A

空服員 **Would you like** something to drink?
[wʊd ju laɪk `sʌmθɪŋ tu drɪŋk]

秀智 Yes, please.
[jɛs pliz]

對話B

空服員 Chicken or beef?
[`tʃɪkɪn ɔr bif]

振洙 Beef, **please.**
[bif pliz]

句型 01 **Would you like + 食物／飲料 ?** 請問你想要～嗎？

這裡用 would 是為了表示禮貌。「would like＋名詞」是客氣地表示「想要～」的句型，如果改成疑問句 Would you like ~? 的話，就成為了「請問你想要～嗎？」的意思。這是客氣地提議某事時用的句型，在飛機上空服員向乘客提供食物或飲料時會很常聽到。

句型 01 請問你要喝點什麼嗎？

句型 02 （請給我）牛肉，謝謝。

01-1

如果搭乘的是外國航空公司的班機，那麼國外旅遊可說是從飛機艙內就開始了。請熟悉在享用飛機餐時，經常聽見及說出口的句型吧！

對話A

空服員 請問你要喝點什麼嗎？

秀智 要，謝謝。

對話B

空服員 （你要）雞肉還是牛肉？

振洙 （請給我）牛肉，謝謝。

新出現的單字

something [`sʌmθɪŋ] 某事物

drink [drɪŋk] 喝

chicken [`tʃɪkɪn] 雞肉

or [ɔr] 或、還是

beef [bif] 牛肉

drink 當作動詞是「喝」，當作名詞則是「飲料」的意思。

句型 02 食物／飲料 , please. （請給我）～，謝謝。

please 有「拜託、麻煩」的意思，不過如果加在名詞後方的話，就成為了「（請給我）～，謝謝。」的意思。因此在接受服務時，如果說「要求的物品＋please.」的話，就成了能夠簡單又尊重地拜託對方的句型。可以在食物或飲料之後加上 please，要求想要的東西；在購物時也可以在顏色或尺寸後加上 please，要求取得該商品。

句型01 練習

請問你想要～嗎？

01-2

◎ 請將單字帶入空格內並說說看。 01-2

Would you like ______?

請問你想要 ______ 嗎？

chicken or beef[1]

[`tʃɪkɪn ɔr bif]

雞肉還是牛肉

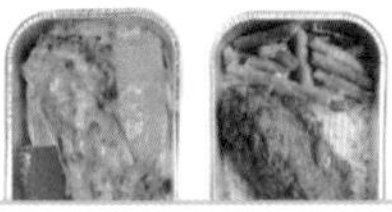

a glass of wine[2]

[ə glæs ɑv waɪn]

一杯葡萄酒

some peanuts

[sʌm `pi͵nʌts]

一些花生

some water

[sʌm `wɔtɚ]

一點水

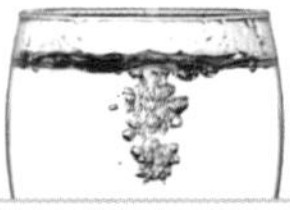

1 chicken or beef or 是「或、還是」的意思，詢問兩個選項中想要哪個的時候，會說 Would you like A or B?。空服員在提供飛機餐時，也經常將問句縮減成 A or B?

2 a glass of wine glass 是「玻璃杯」，「a glass of＋名詞」則是「一杯～」的意思。可以像是 a glass of water（一杯水）, a glass of orange juice（一杯柳橙汁）這樣，在後面帶入各種飲料名稱使用。

句型02 練習

（請給我）～，謝謝。

01-3

◎ 請將單字帶入空格內並說說看。 01-3

＿＿＿, please.

（請給我）＿＿＿，謝謝。

Chicken
[`tʃɪkɪn]
雞肉

Fish
[fɪʃ]
魚

Orange juice
[`ɔrɪndʒ dʒus]
柳橙汁

Coke[1]
[kok]
可樂

Coffee
[`kɔfɪ]
咖啡

A beer
[ə bɪr]
一杯啤酒

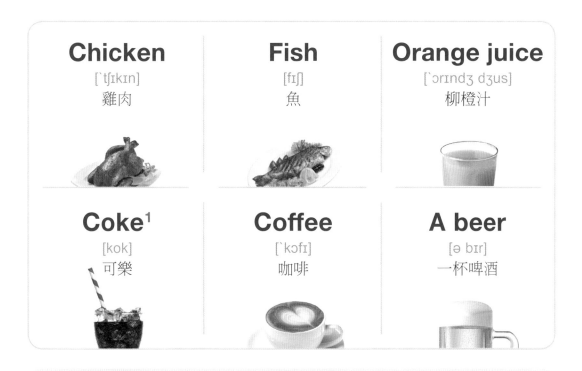

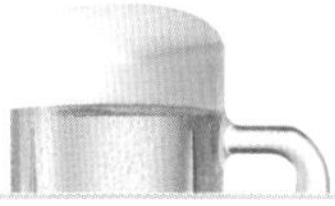

■ **機上提供的飲料** 除了上面提到的飲料之外，其他代表性的機上飲料還有 milk [mɪlk] 牛奶、tea [ti] 紅茶、green tea [grin ti] 綠茶、whisky [`hwɪskɪ] 威士忌等。

1 Coke 可樂是從 Coca-Cola（可口可樂）縮減而來的字，英文是 Coke [kok]。另外，其他公司的飲料產品，也直接叫做 Pepsi [`pɛpsɪ]（百事）。其他汽水也是一樣，只要直接說產品名 7up [`sɛvən ʌp]（七喜）或 Sprite [spraɪt]（雪碧）就可以了。

對話 飛機餐是飛行的亮點

01-4

● 請聽以下對話，並跟著說說看。 01-4

搭乘外國航空公司的班機出國旅行的秀智，終於等到了期待已久的飛機餐時間。

空服員 Beef or fish?
[bif ɔr fɪʃ]

秀智 **Beef, please.**
[bif pliz]

空服員 **Would you like something to drink?**
[wʊd ju laɪk `sʌmθɪŋ tu drɪŋk]

秀智 Yes. What drinks do you have?
[jɛs] [hwɑt drɪŋks du ju hæv]

空服員 We have Coke, Sprite, and orange juice.
[wi hæv kok spraɪt ænd `ɔrɪndʒ dʒus]

Sprite 雪碧

秀智 I'd like a Coke.
[aɪd laɪk ə kok]

空服員 Here you are.
[hɪr ju ɑr]

秀智 Thank you.
[θæŋk ju]

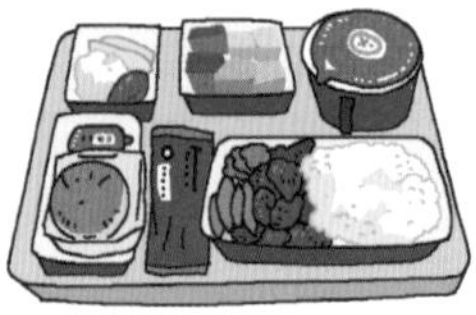

空服員 （你要）牛肉還是魚肉？
秀智 **（請給我）牛肉，謝謝。**
空服員 **請問你要喝點什麼嗎？**
秀智 要，有什麼飲料？
空服員 有可樂、雪碧和柳橙汁。
秀智 （請給我）可樂，謝謝。
空服員 在這裡。
秀智 謝謝。

驗收 01 飛機餐

解答在 214 頁

A 請從選項中選出能填入空格的單字。

選項 **please** **would** **or** **drink**

① 請問你要喝點什麼嗎？

_____ you like something to _____?

② （你要）雞肉還是牛肉？

Chicken _____ beef?

③ （請給我）牛肉，謝謝。

Beef, _____.

B 請在選項中找出適當的字詞，並完成下列句子。

選項 **coke** **some water** **fish** **a glass of wine**

① 請問你想要來一點水嗎？

Would you like _____?

② 請問你想要來一杯葡萄酒嗎？

Would you like _____?

③ （請給我）可樂，謝謝。

_____, please.

④ （請給我）魚，謝謝。

_____, please.

02 機內服務

◎ 請聽以下對話，並跟著說說看。 02-1

對話A

秀智 **Can I get** a blanket?
[kæn aɪ gɛt ə `blæŋkɪt]

空服員 Sure. Here you are.
[ʃʊr] [hɪr ju ɑr]

對話B

振洙 **Could you** take my tray?
[kʊd ju tek maɪ tre]

空服員 Sure.
[ʃʊr]

句型 03 **Can I get + 物品 ?** 可以給我～嗎？

can 表示「可以～」，「Can I＋動詞?」則表示「我可以～嗎？」，在詢問他人能否做某事時使用。動詞 get 是「得到～」的意思，因此 Can I get ~? 直譯的話，就成了「我可以得到～嗎？」。當表示想要某物品時，這個句子則表示「可以給我～嗎？」，有拜託的意思，是在向空服員索取食物、飲料或機上物品時所使用的句型。

句型 03 可以給我一條毯子嗎？

句型 04 能請你收走我的托盤嗎？

02-1

在長途飛行之中，會發生各種要麻煩空服員的事情。一起來學習在飛機內要求服務或拜託某事的時候，所使用的句型吧！

對話A

秀智　可以給我一條毯子嗎？

空服員　當然，在這裡。

對話A

振洙　能請你收走我的托盤嗎？

空服員　當然。

新出現的單字

get [gɛt] 收到、得到

blanket [`blæŋkɪt] 毯子

sure [ʃʊr] 當然的、好的

here [hɪr] 在這裡

take [tek] 帶走、收走

tray [tre] 托盤

Sure 與 Yes（是）是相同的意思，是給予正面回覆時可以使用的字詞。

句型 04 Could you + 動詞 ? 能請你～嗎？

could 與 would 相同，都是表示客氣的用字。「Could you＋動詞?」意為「能請你～嗎？」，是有禮貌地要求他人時可以使用的句型。「Would you＋動詞?」也有相同的意思。若要再更慎重地拜託時，還可以加上 please：「Could [Would] you please＋動詞?」。

句型03 練習　可以給我～嗎？

02-2

◎ 請將單字帶入空格內並說說看。 02-2

Can I get ______ ?

可以給我 ______ 嗎？

a newspaper [ə `njuzˏpepɚ] 一份報紙	**a pen** [ə pɛn] 一枝筆	**a pillow** [ə `pɪlo] 一個枕頭

a sleeping mask [ə `slipɪŋ mæsk] 一副（睡眠用）眼罩	**earplugs**[1] [`ɪrˏplʌgz] 耳塞	**headphones**[1] [`hɛdˏfonz] 耳機

■ **機內提供的物品**　除上述物品外，在飛機上為了乘客的方便，也會提供像 slippers [`slɪpɚz] 拖鞋、magazine [ˏmægə`zin] 雜誌、airsickness bag [`ɛrˏsɪknɪs bæg] 嘔吐袋、medicine [`mɛdəsn] 藥品等多種物品。

1 **earplugs / headphones**　耳塞／耳機因為蓋住耳朵的部分有兩處，所以在單字前面不會加上表示「一個」的 a 或是 an，而必須在結尾加上 s，以複數型態使用。

句型04 練習

能請你～嗎？

02-3

請將單字帶入空格內並說說看。 02-3

Could you ______?

能請你 ______ 嗎？

help me[1]

[hɛlp mi]

幫忙我

wake me for meals

[wek mi fɔr milz]

在用餐時叫醒我

move your seat up

[muv jʊɚ sit ʌp]

豎直椅背

switch seats with me

[swɪtʃ sits wɪð mi]

和我交換位子

1 help me Could you help me 後面加上動詞的話，就能表示「能請你幫我～嗎？」，也可以帶入各種請託的事項，像是 Could you help me find my seat?（能請你幫我找我的座位嗎？）、Could you help me fill out this form?（能請你幫我填寫這張表格嗎？）等。

對話 天空中的親切服務

02-4

請聽以下對話，並跟著說說看。 02-4

振洙享用完餐點了，想要請空服員收走托盤。

振洙 Excuse me.
[ɪkˋskjuz mi]

空服員 Yes. How may I help you?
[jɛs] [haʊ me aɪ hɛlp ju]

振洙 **Could you take my tray?**
[kʊd ju tek maɪ tre]

空服員 Of course.
[ɑv kors]

振洙 Thank you. When will we land?
[θæŋk ju] [hwɛn wɪl wi lænd]

land 降落

空服員 In two hours.
[ɪn tu aʊrz]

振洙 **Can I get a blanket?** It's chilly on the plane.
[kæn aɪ gɛt ə ˋblæŋkɪt] [ɪts ˋtʃɪlɪ ɑn ðə plen]

空服員 I'll bring one right away.
[aɪl brɪŋ wʌn raɪt əˋwe]

chilly 冷颼颼的 right away 馬上

振洙 不好意思。
空服員 是，有什麼能幫忙的嗎？
振洙 **能請你收走我的托盤嗎？**
空服員 當然。
振洙 謝謝。我們什麼時候降落？
空服員 兩個小時之後。
振洙 **可以給我一條毯子嗎？**飛機內有點冷。
空服員 我馬上拿一條過來。

驗收 02 機內服務

解答在 214 頁

A 請從選項中選出能填入空格的單字。

選項 **sure** **tray** **get** **could**

① 可以給我一條毯子嗎？

Can I ______ a blanket?

② 當然。

______.

③ 能請你收走我的托盤嗎？

______ you take my ______?

B 請在選項中找出適當的表達方式，並完成下列句子。

選項 **switch seats with me** **a newspaper** **wake me for meals** **headphones**

① 可以給我一份報紙嗎？

Can I get ______?

② 可以給我耳機嗎？

Can I get ______?

③ 能請你在用餐時叫醒我嗎？

Could you ______?

④ 能請你跟我交換位子嗎？

Could you ______?

02-5

seat number 座位號碼

seat [sit] 是「座位」，而 number [`nʌmbɚ] 是「號碼」的意思。在飛機內的座位號碼通常以數字搭配英文字母呈現，像 26A、26B、26C。一般標示在頭頂上方的行李艙上。

economy class 經濟艙

economy [ɪ`kɑnəmɪ] 是「節約」，而 class [klæs] 表示「等級」，因為經濟艙是最便宜的，一般來說也是最多人搭乘的艙等。機艙內座位雖然會因航空公司或飛機機種有所不同，但通常會以 first class（頭等艙）、business class（商務艙）、economy class（經濟艙）來區分等級。

window / aisle 窗戶 / 走道

window [`wɪndo] 是「窗戶」，aisle [aɪl] 是「通道」的意思。在機內的座位可以分成窗戶邊的 window seat（窗邊座位），與走道邊的 aisle seat（走道座位）。大型飛機的話，也有位在窗邊座位與走道座位之間的 middle seat（中間座位）。

exit 出口

exit [`ɛksɪt] 是「出口」的意思，即在飛機緊急迫降時使用的緊急出口。在緊急出口旁的座位，雖然可以伸腳的空間很寬廣，是舒服的位子，但因為在緊急逃生時必須協助空服員，因此孕婦、長者、殘障人士及兒童不能乘坐。

Fasten seatbelt while seated

坐在座位上時請繫上安全帶

fasten [ˋfæsən] 是「繫」，seatbelt [ˋsitbɛlt] 表示「安全帶」，while [hwaɪl] 是指「在～的期間」，seated [ˋsitɪd] 則表示「坐著」。飛機起降時自然要繫安全帶，而通過亂流時，因為可能會劇烈晃動，所以坐著時也繫上安全帶比較安全。

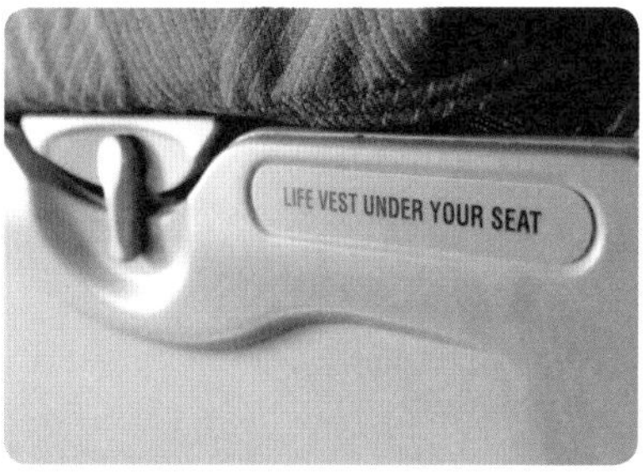

Life vest under your seat

救生衣在座位的下方

life 是「生命」的意思，life vest [laɪf vɛst] 是「救生衣」，也稱為 life jacket [laɪf ˋdʒækɪt]。救生衣是在飛機迫降於水面上時使用的，平時則是放在座位的下方。

lavatory / vacant 化妝室 / 空的

飛機內的化妝室被稱為 lavatory [ˋlævəˌtorɪ]。如果在化妝室門上有 vacant [ˋvekənt]「空的」的標誌的話，只要將門往內推開就可以了；但如果顯示 occupied [ˋɑkjʊpaɪd]「使用中」，就表示裡面有人，必須等待裡面的人出來。

No smoking in lavatory

洗手間內禁菸

smoking [ˋsmokɪŋ] 是「吸菸」的意思，而 No smoking 就是「禁止吸菸」，即「禁菸」的意思。雖然從前在機艙內有可以吸菸的區域，但最近整個機艙都屬於禁菸區域，因此在洗手間內也不可以吸菸。

生動的旅遊資訊

填寫入境卡

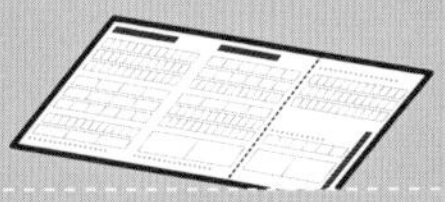

在飛行途中，空服員會將
入境審查時要繳交的入境卡
發給大家。依照國家不同，
形式會有些許的差異。
一起來熟悉填寫入境卡時，
必須要知道的用語吧！

Family name / Surname / Last name 姓

填寫 CHEN（陳）、LIN（林）、HUANG（黃）、CHANG（張）等姓氏。

First name / Given names 名字

填寫 YA-TING（雅婷）、YI-CHUN（怡君）等名字。必須填寫與護照上完全相同的英文名字。

Sex / Gender 性別

Male (M) 男性

Female (F) 女性

Date of birth / Birth date 出生年月日

Day / Month / Year 日／月／年度

在西方國家通常會從小時間的單位開始寫，因此請留意生日年月日的順序必須寫成日／月／年。

Town and country of birth 出生城市及國籍

只要填寫出生的城市及國家名稱即可，例如 TAIPEI, TAIWAN（台北、台灣）。

Nationality 國籍

寫上 REPUBLIC OF CHINA（中華民國）或是 TAIWAN（台灣）即可。

Occupation 職業

OFFICE WORKER（公司職員）、HOUSEWIFE（主婦）、BUSINESSPERSON（商人）等等，寫上自己的職業。

Contact address 連絡住址

寫上已預約的飯店地址。如果是下榻民宿或熟人的家中的情況，只要寫該住家的地址即可。

Passport number 護照號碼

Place of issue 發簽地點

指發出簽證的地方，可能是 TAIWAN（台灣）之外的地方，如 TOKYO（東京）、BANGKOK（曼谷）。

Length of stay 滯留期間

只要像 10 DAYS（10 日）一般，在停留時間的數字後加上 DAYS（日）即可。如果是 10 天 9 夜的行程，只要寫「10 日」就可以了。

Port of last departure 最後出發地

假設是從桃園國際機場出發的話，請寫 TAIPEI（台北）或機場代碼 TPE。若中途有轉機，則要寫到達目的地前的最後一個出發地。

Flight number 航班號碼

Signature 署名，簽名

入境時

03 入境審查

04 領取行李

03 入境審查

◎ 請聽以下對話，並跟著說說看。 03-1

對話A

移民官 What is the purpose of your visit?
[hwɑt ɪz ðə `pɝpəs ɑv jʊɚ `vɪzɪt]

振洙 **I'm here** for sightseeing.
[aɪm hɪr fɔr `saɪt͵siɪŋ]

對話B

移民官 How long will you be staying?
[haʊ lɔŋ wɪl ju bi `steɪŋ]

秀智 **I plan to stay for** ten days.
[aɪ plæn tu ste fɔr tɛn dez]

句型 05 **I'm here +** 入境理由 我來這裡～。

I'm 是 I am 的縮寫，可表示「我是～」、「我在～」等狀態，這裡加上表示「（在）這裡」的 here，形成 I'm here，表示「我在這裡」。此時若後面接了以介系詞 for、on 帶出的「入境理由」，就有「我是因為～而在這裡」的意思，即「為了～來這裡」，可表示來訪目的。另外，詢問入境理由時，也會聽到 What brings you here?（是什麼把你帶來這裡？／你為什麼來這裡？）。

句型 05 我來這裡觀光。

句型 06 我計畫待十天。

03-1

下了飛機之後，想進入另一個國家，就一定要通過入境審查。來學著回答最常被問到的問題——入境目的及停留時間的表達方式吧！

對話A

移民官 你來訪的目的是什麼?

振洙 我來這裡觀光。

對話B

移民官 你打算待多久？

振洙 我計畫待十天。

新出現的單字

purpose [`pɝpəs] 目的

visit [`vɪzɪt] 拜訪

sightseeing [`saɪt͵siɪŋ] 觀光

stay [ste] 停留

plan [plæn] 計畫

ten [tɛn] 十

day [de] 日、天

句型 06 I plan to stay for + 一段時間 我計畫待～。

這是在回答關於停留時間的問題時，可以活用的句型。「plan to＋動詞」表示「計畫做～」，可用來說明未來的計劃或行程。stay 是意為「停留、待」的動詞，for 在這裡用來表示「持續～（時間）」。也可以省略 I plan to stay，僅簡單地回答 For ten days.（待十天）。

句型05 練習

我來這裡～。

03-2

請將單字帶入空格內並說說看。 03-2

I'm here ______.

我來這裡 ______ 。

on vacation
[ɑn veˋkeʃən]
度假

on business
[ɑn ˋbɪznɪs]
出差

to visit my friend[1]
[tu ˋvɪzɪt maɪ frɛnd]
拜訪朋友

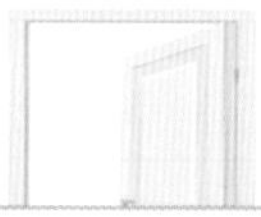

to study English
[tu ˋstʌdɪ ˋɪŋglɪʃ]
學英文

1 to visit my friend 如果寫成〈I'm here to＋動詞〉的話，就是「我來這裡做～」的意思。visit 作為動詞是「拜訪」的意思，除了 friend（朋友）之外，也可以放入自己打算在國外見的人，表示「為了拜訪～而來」。請試著在 my [maɪ]（我的）之後放入 relatives [ˋrɛlətɪv]「親戚」、family [ˋfæməlɪ]「家族」、daughter [ˋdɔtɚ]「女兒」、son [sʌn]「兒子」等各式各樣的單字並練習說說看。

句型06 練習

我計畫待～。

03-3

◎ 請將單字帶入空格內並說說看。 03-3

I plan to stay for ______.

我計畫待 ______ 。

three days
[θri dez]
三天

a week
[ə wik]
一週

two week
[tu wiks]
兩週

a month
[ə mʌnθ]
一個月

two months
[tu mʌnθs]
兩個月

about ten days[1]
[ə`baʊt tɛn dez]
大約十天

■ **表達一段時間的方式** 數字後面加上 day [de]「日」、week [wik]「週」、month [mʌnθ]「月」，就可以表達「一段時間」。不過，當數字是 2 以上時，就必須要在單字後加上 s，使用複數型，像 days [dez]、weeks [wiks]、months [mʌnθs]。

1 about ten days about 是「～左右」的意思。當說的不是準確的一段時間，而是大概的時間段時，請在數字的前面加上 about。

對話　令人心臟撲通跳的入境審查

03-4

請聽以下對話，並跟著說說看。 03-4

秀智懷抱著緊張的心情等待入境審查，終於輪到她了。

移民官　Your passport, please.
[jʊɚ　`pæsˌport　pliz]

passport 護照

秀智　Here you are.
[hɪr　ju　ɑr]

移民官　What brings you here?
[hwɑt　brɪŋz　ju　hɪr]

bring 帶來

秀智　**I'm here for sightseeing.**
[aɪm　hɪr　fɔr　`saɪtˌsiɪŋ]

移民官　How long do you intend to stay?
[haʊ　lɔŋ　du　ju　ɪn`tɛnd　tu　ste]

intend 意圖，打算

秀智　**I plan to stay for ten days.**
[aɪ　plæn　tu　ste　fɔr　tɛn　dez]

移民官　Where will you stay?
[hwɛr　wɪl　ju　ste]

秀智　I will stay at the Marriott Hotel.
[aɪ　wɪl　ste　æt　ðə　ˈmæriˌɑt　ho`tɛl]

移民官　（請給我）你的護照，謝謝。
秀智　在這裡。
移民官　你為什麼會來這裡？
秀智　**我來這裡觀光。**
移民官　你打算在這裡待多久？
秀智　**我計畫待十天。**
移民官　你會住哪裡？
秀智　我會住在 Marriott 飯店。

驗收 03 入境審查

解答在 214 頁

A 請從選項中選出能填入空格的單字。

選項 purpose | plan | sightseeing | stay

① 我來這裡觀光。

I'm here for ______.

② 我計畫待十天。

I ______ to ______ for ten days.

③ 你來訪的目的是什麼？

What is the ______ of your visit?

B 請在選項中找出適當的表達方式，並完成下列句子。

選項 a week | to visit my friend | on vacation | about ten days

① 我來這裡拜訪朋友。

I'm here ______.

② 我來這裡度假

I'm here ______.

③ 我計畫待一週。

I plan to stay for ______.

④ 我計畫待十天左右。

I plan to stay for ______.

04 領取行李

◎ 請聽以下對話，並跟著說說看。 04-1

對話A

服務人員 **What's your** flight number?
[hwɑts jʊɚ flaɪt `nʌmbɚ]

秀智 KE 123.
[ke i wʌn tu θri]

對話B

服務人員 **Do you have** your baggage claim ticket?
[du ju hæv jʊɚ `bægɪdʒ klem `tɪkɪt]

振洙 Yes. Here you are.
[jɛs] [hɪr ju ɑr]

句型 07 What's your + 名詞 ? 你的～是什麼？

What's 是 What is 的縮寫，表示「～是什麼？」，your 則表示「你的」，因此 What's your ~? 就是「你的～是什麼？」的意思。當要詢問與對方相關的資訊或個人資料（如姓名、地址、電話號碼等）時，可以使用這個句型，入境審查時也會經常聽到。

句型 07 你的航班號碼是什麼（幾號）？

句型 08 你有行李託運存根嗎？

04-1

結束入境審查後，就可以在行李轉盤上領取託運的行李了。現在就來學會從服務人員那裡聽到，與領行李相關的句型吧！

對話 A

服務人員　你的航班號碼是什麼（幾號）？

秀智　是 KE123。

對話 B

服務人員　你有行李託運存根嗎？

振洙　有的，在這裡。

新出現的單字

flight [flaɪt] 航班

number [`nʌmbə] 數字、號碼

baggage [`bægɪdʒ] 行李

claim [klem] 認領、要求、索取

ticket [`tɪkɪt] 票、存根、標籤

baggage claim ticket 是領取行李時方便確認的票據存根。在辦理登機手續時，地勤會在行李及登機證後面各貼上一張附有條碼的貼紙，以便存查。

句型 08 Do you have + 名詞 ? 你有～嗎？

have 是「擁有～」的意思，疑問句 Do you have ~? 則表示「你有～嗎？」。這是要確認對方的持有物時所使用的句型，在安全檢查或海關會經常聽到。回答時，只要說 Yes, I do.（是的，我有。）或是 No, I don't.（不，我沒有。）就可以了。

句型07 練習

你的～是什麼？

04-2

請將單字帶入空格內並說說看。 04-2

What's your ______?

你的 ______ 是什麼？

name[1]
[nem]
姓名

home address
[hom `ædrɛs]
住家地址

nationality
[ˌnæʃə`nælətɪ]
國籍

phone number
[fon `nʌmbɚ]
電話號碼（幾號）

seat number
[sit `nʌmbɚ]
座位號碼（幾號）

final destination
[`faɪnəl ˌdɛstə`neʃən]
最終目的地（在哪裡）

1 name 雖然中文姓名是「陳怡君」一樣以「姓＋名」的順序來表示，不過在英文中會顛倒過來，變成 Yi-Chun Chen（怡君 陳）這樣以「名＋姓」的順序來表達。名字是 first name [fɝst nem]「在前面的名字」，或稱為 given name [`gɪvən nem]「（由父母親）給予的名字」，姓則是 last name [læst nem]「最後面的名字」、family name [`fæməlɪ nem]「家族名字」，也可稱為 surname [`sɝˌnem]「姓」。

句型08
練習

你有～嗎？

04-3

請將單字帶入空格內並說說看。 04-3

Do you have ______?

你有 ______ 嗎？

any liquids
[`ɛnɪ `lɪkwɪdz]
（任何）液體

any sharp objects
[`ɛnɪ ʃarp `ɑbdʒɪkts]
（任何）尖銳物品

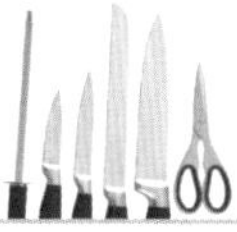

any carry-on bags
[`ɛnɪ `kærɪˏɑn bægz]
（任何）手提行李

anything to declare[1]
[`ɛnɪˏθɪŋ tu dɪ`klɛr]
（任何）須向海關申報的物品

■ **any** any 在疑問句中有「任何、一些」的意思。在 any 後面加上名詞的話，並不一定會翻譯出 any 的意思。

1 **anything to declare** declare 是「申報（關稅）」的意思。領好行李出去時，就會看見海關，根據入境國家的規定不同，只要在需申報關稅的情況下申報即可。如果沒有需要申報的物品，請說 No, I have nothing to declare「不，我沒有要申報的東西」。

對話 尋找行李三萬里

04-4

◎ 請聽以下對話，並跟著說說看。 04-4

通過入境審查後的振洙，正踏著輕盈的腳步前去領取行李。

振洙 Where is the baggage claim area?
[hwɛr ɪz ðə `bægɪdʒ klem `ɛrɪə]

服務人員 **What's your flight number?**
[hwɑts jʊɚ flaɪt `nʌmbɚ]

振洙 OZ 234.
[o zi tu θri for]

服務人員 You can pick up your luggage on carrousel number 7. It's over there.
[ju kæn pɪk ʌp jʊɚ `lʌgɪdʒ ɑn ˏkærʊ`zɛl `nʌmbɚ`sɛvən] [ɪts `ovɚ ðɛr]

carrousel 行李轉盤

振洙怎麼等都沒在行李輸送帶上看到自己的行李，擔心的他便向服務人員詢問。

振洙 Excuse me. I can't find my luggage.
[ɪk`skjuz mi ] [ aɪ kænt faɪnd maɪ `lʌgɪdʒ]

服務人員 **Do you have your baggage claim ticket?**
[du ju hæv jʊɚ `bægɪdʒ klem `tɪkɪt]

振洙 Yes. Here it is.
[jɛs] [hɪr ɪt ɪz]

振洙 行李提領區在哪裡？
服務人員 **你的航班號碼是什麼（幾號）？**
振洙 是 OZ 234。
服務人員 你可以在 7 號轉盤領取你的行李。在那邊。

振洙 不好意思，我找不到我的行李。
服務人員 **你有行李託運存根嗎？**
振洙 有的，在這裡。

驗收 04 領取行李

解答在 215 頁

A 請從選項中選出能填入空格的單字。

選項 **here** | **number** | **have** | **claim**

① 你的航班號碼是什麼（幾號）？

What's your flight ______?

② 你有行李託運存根嗎？

Do you ______ your baggage ______ ticket?

③ 在這裡。

______ you are.

B 請在選項中找出適當的表達方式，並完成下列句子。

選項 **any liquids** | **name** | **anything to declare** | **home address**

① 你的名字是什麼？

What's your ______?

② 你的住家地址是什麼？

What's your ______?

③ 你有（任何）液體嗎？

Do you have ______?

④ 你有（任何）須向海關申報的物品嗎？

Do you have ______?

尋找英文吧！入境（抵達機場） 04-5

04-5

Arrival 抵達／入境

抵達最終目的地並下了飛機之後，只要跟著 Arrival [əˋraɪvəl]（抵達／入境）的標誌移動就可以了。相反的，如果是要搭乘飛機回國時，只要跟著 Departure [dɪˋpɑrtʃɚ]（出發／出境）即可。

Transfer 轉乘

若不是搭乘直航班機，而是必須轉搭其他飛機，請跟著寫有 Transfer [trænsˋfɝ]（轉機）或 Flight connections [flaɪt kəˋnɛkʃən]（轉接班機）的標誌移動。可以在機場的電子螢幕上，確認接下來班機的登機口。

Passport control
護照審查（證照審查）

passport 是「護照」，control 是「管制、檢查」的意思，passport control [ˋpæsˏport kənˋtrol] 就是我們給出護照、接受出入境證照審查的「護照審查站」的意思。只要提早準備好護照和入境卡，接受入境審查即可。

Visitor 訪客

接受入境審查時，請移動到 Visitors [ˋvɪzɪtɚz]（訪客）、Non-citizen [nɑn ˋsɪtəzən]（非公民）、Foreigner [ˋfɔrɪnɚ]（外國人）區域等待。如果是在英國等歐洲國家的話，則請不要到 EU Passports（歐盟護照）區域，而要到 All other passports（其他所有護照）區域等待。

Baggage claim 行李提領

baggage 是「行李」，claim 是「認領、要求、索取」的意思，可以領取託運行李的地方，就稱為 Baggage claim [`bægɪdʒ klem]。在英國則是稱為 Baggage reclaim [`bægɪdʒ rɪ`klem]。

Customs control 海關檢查檯

customs [`kʌstəmz] 是「海關」的意思。在海關檢查檯繳交機上寫好的海關申報單，通常就能直接通行。只有行李很多或是看起來很怪的時候，才需要另外接受檢查。如果沒有這種情況，直接前往入境大廳就可以了。

Trains / Buses 火車／公車

從機場移動到市區時，請認清 Train [tren]（火車）、Bus [bʌs]（公車）、Shuttle [`ʃʌtəl]（接駁車）、Taxi [`tæksɪ]（計程車）等指示牌，尋找要搭乘的交通工具。在不同的英語區國家，表示地下鐵的字不同，有 Subway [`sʌb͵we]、Metro [`mɛtro]、Underground [`ʌndɚ͵graʊnd]。

Rent-a-car 租車

在機場有許多可以租借車輛的租車業者。rent 是「租借」，car 是「汽車」的意思，rent-a-car [rɛnt ə kɑr] 是租賃汽車，也就是「租車」的意思。也會寫成 Car rental [kɑr `rɛntəl]。

生動的旅遊資訊

填寫海關申報單

入境通過海關時，
必須要繳交海關申報單。
像入境卡一樣
寫好個人資訊後，
讀過內容並勾選
YES（是）或 NO（不是）即可。

Number of Family members traveling with you
與你同行的家族成員人數

U.S. Street Address (hotel name/destination)
美國地址（飯店名稱／目的地）

Passport issued by (country)
護照發照（國家）

Passport number 護照號碼

Country of Residence 居住國家

Countries visited on this trip prior to U.S. arrival
抵達美國前到訪的國家

Airline / Flight No.
航空公司／班機號碼

I am bringing
我本人攜帶（以下項目）

(a) **fruits, vegetables, plants, seeds, food, insects**
水果、蔬菜、植物、種子、食品、昆蟲

(b) **meats, animals, animal/wildlife products**
肉類、動物、動物／野生動物製品

(c) **disease agent, cell cultures, snails** 病原體、細胞培養物、蝸牛

(d) **soil or have been on a farm**
土壤、或曾去過農場

I have been in close proximity of livestock.
本人曾與家畜緊密生活。

I am carrying currency or monetary instruments over $10,000 U.S. or foreign equivalent.
本人持有一萬以上美元之等值的外幣現金或貨幣工具。

VISITORS-the total value of all articles that will remain in the U.S., including commercial merchandise is:
訪客：包含商業性物品，將留在美國境內的物品總價值：

搭乘交通工具時

05 公車

06 計程車

07 地下鐵

05 公車

◎ 請聽以下對話，並跟著說說看。 05-1

對話A

振洙 **Which bus goes to** Times Square?

[hwɪtʃ bʌs goz tu taɪmz skwɛr]

行人 The number 10 bus.

[ðə ˋnʌmbɚ tɛn bʌs]

對話B

振洙 **Does this bus go to** Times Square?

[dʌz ðɪs bʌs go tu taɪmz skwɛr]

公車司機 No. You should take the number 10 bus.

[no] [ju ʃʊd tek ðə ˋnʌmbɚ tɛn bʌs]

句型 09 **Which bus goes to +** 地點 **?** 哪班公車會到～？

which 表示「哪種的、哪個」，which bus 則表示「哪輛公車」。在「去～」的句子裡，中文和英文的語序一樣，是說「去（動詞）＋地點」，因此可以在動詞 goes to 的後面帶入地點，詢問公車是否開往欲前往的目的地。

句型 09 哪班公車會到時代廣場？

句型 10 這班公車會到時代廣場嗎？

05-1

搭乘公車可以一面欣賞窗外風景一面旅行，因此是經常被利用的大眾交通運輸工具。來認識詢問公車是否前往要去的目的地，及確認公車目的地的表達方式吧！

對話 A

振洙 哪班公車會到時代廣場？

行人 10 號公車。

對話 B

振洙 這班公車會到時代廣場嗎？

公車司機 不會，你得搭 10 號公車才行。

新出現的單字

which [hwɪtʃ] 哪種的、哪個

bus [bʌs] 公車

square [skwɛr] 廣場

should [ʃʊd] 必須、應該

take [tek] 搭乘（交通工具）

Times Square 是時代廣場，或稱時報廣場，位於百老匯大道與第七大道的交會處，美國紐約著名的觀光景點。口語上聽到的發音很像兩個單字相連 [ˋtaɪmskwɛr]。

句型 10 Does this bus go to + 地點 ? 這班公車會到～嗎？

這是要向公車司機確認公車是否開往欲前往的目的地時，可以使用的句型。只要在 Does this bus go to ~ 後面，帶入自己打算去的地點名稱就可以了。this bus 表示「這班公車」，若是在公車站牌指著遠處的公車，詢問該公車是否前往目的地時，請用 that [ðæt]（那）取代 this（這），以 Does that bus go to ~? 來詢問。

句型09 練習　哪班公車會到～？

05-2

● 請將單字帶入空格內並說說看。 05-2

Which bus goes to ______?

哪班公車會到 ______ ？

the concert hall

[ðə `kɑnsɚt hɔl]

演奏廳、音樂廳

the baseball stadium

[ðə `besˌbɔl `stedɪəm]

棒球場

the British Museum[1]

[ðə `brɪtɪʃ mju`zɪəm]

大英博物館

Victoria Station

[vɪk`torɪə `steʃən]

維多利亞站

1 the British Museum　大英博物館位於英國倫敦，是世界最大的博物館之一。British 表示「英國的」，museum 則表示「博物館」。這裡展示了古埃及、希臘、中國等世界各國的各種文物。因為有許多文物是英國在帝國主義時期，從世界各國帶回的，所以引發了所有權的爭議：希臘要求歸還帕德嫩神殿的雕刻便是具代表性的例子。

句型10 練習

這班公車會到～嗎？

05-3

請將單字帶入空格內並說說看。 05-3

Does this bus go to ______ ?

這班公車會到 ______ 嗎？

Wall Street[1]
[wɔl strit]
華爾街

Fifth Avenue[1]
[fɪfθ ˋævə͵nju]
第五大道

City Hall
[ˋsɪtɪ hɔl]
市政府

Chicago
[ʃəˋkɑgo]
芝加哥

Manly Beach
[ˋmænlɪ bitʃ]
曼利海灘

Chinatown[2]
[ˋtʃaɪnə͵taʊn]
中國城

1 **Wall Street / Fifth Avenue** street 和 avenue 都有「街道、路」的意思，是用在道路名稱上的單字。在紐約，street 指東西向的道路，avenue 則指南北向的道路。

2 **Chinatown** China 表示「中國」，town 則表示「市鎮」，所以 Chinatown 顧名思義就是指中國人生活的「中國城」。美國洛杉磯的中國城，人口超過四萬，規模非常大，區域內中餐廳及其他店家的密度也很高。

對話 一個人的公車旅行

05-4

◎ 請聽以下對話，並跟著說說看。 05-4

秀智正在公車站牌找去時代廣場的公車。

秀智 Excuse me. **Which bus goes to Times Square?**
[ɪk`skjuz mi] [hwɪtʃ bʌs goz tu taɪmz skwɛr]

行人 Take the number 10 bus.
[tek ðə `nʌmbɚ tɛn bʌs]

秀智 Thank you.
[θæŋk ju]

過了一下，秀智坐上了 10 號公車。

秀智 **Does this bus go to Times Square?**
[dʌz ðɪs bʌs go tu taɪmz skwɛr]

公車司機 Yes, it does.
[jɛs ɪt dʌz]

秀智 Please tell me when we get there.
[pliz tɛl mi hwɛn wi gɛt ðɛr]

公車司機 Okay. I'll let you know.
[ˏo`ke] [aɪl lɛt ju no]

秀智 不好意思，**哪班車會到時代廣場？**
行人 請搭 10 號公車。
秀智 謝謝。

秀智 **這班車會到時代廣場嗎？**
公車司機 是，會去。
秀智 到了那裡的話，請告訴我。
公車司機 好，我會讓你知道（告訴你）。

驗收 05 公車

解答在 215 頁

A 請從選項中選出能填入空格的單字。

選項 **number** | **which** | **go** | **take**

① 哪班公車會到時代廣場？

[ ] bus goes to Times Square?

② 這班公車會到時代廣場嗎？

Does this bus [ ] to Times Square?

③ 你得搭 10 號公車。

You should [ ] the [ ] 10 bus.

B 請在選項中找出適當的表現，並完成下列句子。

選項 **Fifth Avenue** | **the baseball stadium** | **Victoria Station** | **City Hall**

① 哪班公車會到維多利亞車站？

Which bus goes to [ ]?

② 哪班公車會到棒球場？

Which bus goes to [ ]?

③ 這班公車會到第五大道嗎？

Does this bus go to [ ]?

④ 這班公車會到市政府嗎？

Does this bus go to [ ]?

06 計程車

請聽以下對話，並跟著說說看 06-1

對話A

計程車司機 Where can I take you?
[hwɛr kæn aɪ tek ju]

秀智 **Could you take me to** the Sun Hotel?
[kʊd ju tek mi tu ðə sʌn ho`tɛl]

對話B

振洙 **How long does it take to get to** the hotel?
[haʊ lɔŋ dʌz ɪt tek tu gɛt tu ðə ho`tɛl]

計程車司機 It takes about 30 minutes.
[ɪt teks ə`baʊt `θɝtɪ `mɪnɪts]

句型 11 Could you take me to + 地點 ?

可以請你帶我去～嗎？

向計程車司機說明目的地時，只要在有禮地拜託他人的句型「Could you＋動詞?」中，帶入動詞 take（帶去、帶領），構成 Could you take me to ~?（你可以帶我去～嗎？）就可以了。另外，也可以利用前面學過的 please，簡單地說「To＋地點, please.」。

句型 11 可以請你帶我去 Sun 飯店嗎？

句型 12 到飯店要花多久時間？

06-1

當行程很緊湊或是身體疲累時，雖然費用較高，但搭乘計程車是相當便利的。來學習告知計程車司機目的地，和詢問抵達目的地要花多久時間的表達方式吧！

對話 A

計程車司機　你要去哪裡？

秀智　可以請你帶我去 Sun 飯店嗎？

對話 B

振洙　到飯店要花多久時間？

計程車司機　大約要花 30 分鐘。

新出現的單字

take [tek] 帶（人）去、花費（時間）

how long [haʊ lɔŋ] 多久

get [gɛt] 抵達

about [ə`baʊt] 大約

thirty [`θɝtɪ] 三十

minute [`mɪnɪt] 分

句型 12 How long does it take to get to+ 地點 ?

到～要花多久時間？

How long 表示「多久」，是詢問時間的字詞。動詞 take 有許多意思，這裡用作「花費（時間）」。因此「How long does it take to＋動詞?」可用來詢問做某件事情所要花費的時間。此時動詞的地方帶入意為「抵達～」的「get to＋地點」的話，就可用來詢問到達目的地所需時間。

句型11 練習

可以請你帶我去～嗎？

06-2

請將單字帶入空格內並說說看。 06-2

Could you take me to ______?

可以請你帶我去 ______ 嗎？

this address

[ðɪs `ædrɛs]

這個地址

Sydney Tower[1]

[`sɪdnɪ `taʊɚ]

雪梨塔

the GE Building[2]

[dʒi i `bɪldɪŋ]

GE（奇異）大樓

Tower Bridge

[`taʊɚ brɪdʒ]

倫敦塔橋

1 Sydney Tower tower 表示「塔」，且主要指有觀景台的高聳建築物。巴黎的 Eiffel Tower [`aɪfəl `taʊɚ]（艾菲爾鐵塔，即巴黎鐵塔）就特別有名。

2 the GE Building 原本的名字是 General Electric Building [`dʒɛnərəl ɪ`lɛktrɪk `bɪldɪŋ]，取開頭字母簡稱為 GE Building，building 是「大樓、建築物」的意思。這棟大樓位於紐約，是一棟約 70 層樓的建築物，發明家愛迪生所創立的通用電氣公司（奇異）就位在這裡。

到～要花多久時間？

06-3

◎ 請將單字帶入空格內並說說看。 06-3

How long does it take to get to the ______?

到 ______ 要花多久時間？

airport
[`ɛrˏport]
機場

bus station[1]
[bʌs `steʃən]
巴士轉運站

university
[ˏjunə`vɝsətɪ]
大學

beach
[bitʃ]
海邊

mall[2]
[mɔl]
購物中心

city center
[`sɪtɪ `sɛntɚ]
市中心

1 bus station 可以搭乘長途巴士的巴士轉運站稱為 bus station [bʌs `steʃən]。另外，因為長途巴士在英國叫作 coach [kotʃ]，所以也稱為 coach station [kotʃ `steʃən]。

2 mall 聚集了各種商家的購物中心是 shopping mall [`ʃɑpɪŋ mɔl]，但簡稱為 mall 也可以，或稱為 shopping center [`ʃɑpɪŋ `sɛntɚ]。

對話 快速又便利的計程車

06-4

◎ 請聽以下對話，並跟著說說看。 06-4

因為觀光行程而疲倦得不得了的秀智，打算回飯店而攔了計程車。

計程車司機 Where are you going?
[hwɛr ɑr ju \`goɪŋ]

秀智 **Could you take me to the Sun Hotel?**
[kʊd ju tek mi tu ðə sʌn ho\`tɛl]

計程車司機 Sure.
[ʃʊr]

秀智 **How long does it take to get to the hotel?**
[haʊ lɔŋ dʌz ɪt tek tu gɛt tu ðə ho\`tɛl]

計程車司機 It usually takes about 20 minutes.
[ɪt \`juʒʊəlɪ teks ə\`baʊt \`twɛntɪ \`mɪnɪts]

usually 通常

車子在飯店前面因為紅綠燈號誌而停下，秀智向司機要求早點下車。

秀智 Can you stop here, please?
[kæn ju stɑp hɪr pliz]

計程車司機 Okay. The total is 25 dollars.
[ˌo\`ke ] [ ðə \`totəl ɪz \`twɛntɪfaɪv \`dɑlɚz]

total 總數

秀智 Keep the change.
[kip ðə tʃendʒ]

change 零錢

計程車司機 你要去哪裡？
秀智 **可以請你帶我去 Sun 飯店嗎？**
計程車司機 當然。
秀智 **到飯店要花多久時間？**
計程車司機 通常要花大約 20 分鐘。

秀智 可以在這裡停車嗎？
計程車司機 好喔。總共 25 美金。
秀智 不用找零了。

驗收 06 計程車

答案在 216 頁

A 請從選項中選出能填入空格的單字。

選項 long | take | minutes | get

① 到飯店要花多久時間？

How ______ does it take to ______ to the hotel?

② 可以請你帶我去 Sun 飯店嗎？

Could you ______ me to the Sun Hotel?

③ 大約要花 30 分鐘。

It takes about 30 ______.

B 請在選項中找出適當的表現，並完成下列句子。

選項 airport | beach | this address | Tower Bridge

① 可以請你帶我到這個地址嗎？

Could you take me to ______?

② 可以請你帶我到倫敦塔橋嗎？

Could you take me to ______?

③ 到機場要花多久時間？

How long does it take to get to the ______?

④ 到海灘要花多久時間？

How long does it take to get to the ______?

07 地下鐵

◎ 請聽以下對話，並跟著說說看。 07-1

對話A

秀智 **Do you know where** the ticket office **is**?
[du ju no hwɛr ðə ˋtɪkɪt ˋɔfɪs ɪz]

行人 It's downstairs.
[ɪts ˏdaʊnˋstɛrz]

對話B

職員 Can I help you?
[kæn aɪ hɛlp ju]

振洙 **I need** a one-day pass.
[aɪ nid ə wʌn de pæs]

句型 13 **Do you know where + 地點 + is?**

你知道～在哪裡嗎？

要問某地點在哪裡時，可以簡單地說「Where is＋地點?」。但就像中文一樣，以「你知道～在哪裡嗎？」提問，會比直接問「～在哪裡？」更婉轉，所以在句子前加上 Do you know（你知道～嗎），會聽起來更謙和有禮。不過，因為這裡的疑問句附屬於其他句子，所以注意語順要改為「where＋地點＋is」。

句型 13 **你知道售票處在哪裡嗎？**

句型 14 **我需要一張一日票。**

07-1

在紐約、倫敦、多倫多等大都市，因為有地下鐵，所以在市區內移動非常方便。來學習搭乘地下鐵或火車時可以使用的句子吧！

對話A

秀智　你知道售票處在哪裡嗎？

行人　在樓下。

對話B

職員　需要幫忙嗎？

振洙　我需要一張一日票。

新出現的單字

know [no] 知道

ticket office [ˋtɪkɪt ˋɔfɪs] 售票處

downstairs [ˌdaʊnˋstɛrz] 樓下

need [nid] 需要

one-day pass [wʌn de pæs] 一日票

句型 14 **I need + 物品 .** 我需要～。

need 是意為「需要～」的動詞。I need 後面帶入自己所需要的物品，就能簡單完成「我需要～」的句型。當物品是可數的名詞時，請在前面加上表示「一個」的 a [ə]、an [æn] 或其他數詞。這是個在售票處買票時很有用的句型，可以像 I need two bus tickets to New York.（我需要兩張去紐約的巴士票）一樣完成句子。

句型13 練習

你知道～在哪裡嗎？

07-2

請將單字帶入空格內並說說看。 07-2

Do you know where ______ is?

你知道 ______ 在哪裡嗎？

the ticket machine[1]
[ðə `tɪkɪt mə`ʃin]
自動售票機

Platform 1
[`plæt͵fɔrm wʌn]
1 號月台

the elevator
[ði `ɛlə͵vetɚ]
電梯

the luggage locker area[2]
[ðə `lʌgɪdʒ `lɑkɚ `ɛrɪə]
置物櫃區

1 **the ticket machine** ticket 是「票」，machine 則是「機器」，因此 ticket machine 就是乘客直接把錢投入後，購買票券的「自動售票機」。

2 **the luggage locker area** luggage 是「行李」，locker 是「（附有鎖的）寄物櫃」，area 則是「區域、地區」。因為寄物櫃通常是好幾個放在一起，所以建議使用複數型。可以用 Do you know where the luggage lockers are? 來詢問他人。

句型14 練習

我需要一個／張～。

07-3

請將單字帶入空格內並說說看。 07-3

I need a ______.

我需要一個／張 ______ 。

one-way ticket[1]

[ˋwʌnˏwe ˋtɪkɪt]

單程票

round-trip ticket[1]

[ˋraʊndˏtrɪp ˋtɪkɪt]

來回票

subway map

[ˋsʌbˏwe mæp]

地下鐵地圖

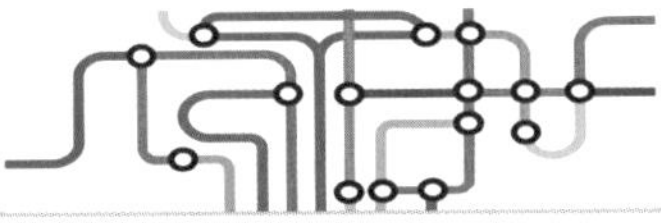

MetroCard[2]

[ˋmɛtroˏkɑrd]

MetroCard

（類似台灣的悠遊卡、一卡通）

1 **one-way ticket / round-trip ticket** 在英國則是完全不同的字，單程票稱為 single ticket [ˋsɪŋgəl ˋtɪkɪt]，來回票稱為 return ticket [rɪˋtɝn ˋtɪkɪt]。

2 **MetroCard** 就算是在同一個國家，不同城市使用的交通卡，名稱也會不同。MetroCard 是紐約所使用的交通卡，在舊金山則是使用 Clipper card [ˋklɪpɚ kɑrd]。另外，倫敦的交通卡是 Oyster card [ˋɔɪstɚ kɑrd]，雪梨則是使用 Opal card [ˋopəl kɑrd]。

對話 購買地下鐵票

07-4

請聽以下對話，並跟著說說看 07-4

進到地鐵站的振洙，正在找售票處。

振洙 Excuse me. **Do you know where the ticket office is**?
[ɪk`skjuz mi ] [ du ju no hwɛr ðə `tɪkɪt `ɔfɪs ɪz]

行人 Over there. Just follow that sign.
[`ovə ðɛr ] [ dʒʌst `fɑlo ðæt saɪn]

follow 跟隨 **sign** 標誌

振洙 Thank you.
[θæŋk ju]

到了售票處的振洙，打算要買可以在一天之內自由乘車的一日票。

振洙 Hello. **I need a one-day pass.** How much is it?
[hə`lo] [aɪ nid ə wʌn de pæs] [haʊ mʌtʃ ɪz ɪt]

職員 It's 7 dollars.
[ɪts `sɛvən`dɑləz]

振洙 Here you are.
[hɪr ju ɑr]

職員 Okay. Here is your pass.
[ˏo`ke] [hɪr ɪz jʊə pæs]

pass 通行券、票

振洙 不好意思，**你知道售票處在哪裡嗎？**
行人 在那邊。跟著那個標誌就好。
振洙 謝謝。

振洙 哈囉，**我需要一張一日票。**多少錢？
職員 7 美金。
振洙 在這邊。
職員 好喔。這裡是你的車票。

驗收 07 地下鐵

答案在 216 頁

A 請從選項中選出能填入空格的單字。

選項 **pass** | **downstairs** | **ticket** | **know**

① 你知道售票處在哪裡嗎？

Do you ______ where the ______ office is?

② 我需要一張一日票。

I need a one-day ______.

③ 在樓下。

It's ______.

B 請在選項中找出適當的表現，並完成下列句子。

選項 **the ticket machine** | **the elevator** | **one-way ticket** | **subway map**

① 你知道電梯在哪裡嗎？

Do you know where ______ is?

② 你知道自動售票機在哪裡嗎？

Do you know where ______ is?

③ 我需要一張單程票。

I need a ______.

④ 我需要一張地下鐵地圖。

I need a ______.

07-5

ground transportation

地面交通工具

ground 具有「地上、土地」的意思，transportation 則是「交通」，因此由兩個單字結合所形成的 ground transportation [graʊnd ˏtrænspɚ`teʃən] 就是指在地面上行駛的計程車、公車、火車等交通工具。

station 車站

station 是指火車或長途巴士定期停靠的車站，規模較大，地鐵站是 subway station [`sʌbˏwe `steʃən]，火車站是 train station [tren `steʃən]，長途巴士站則是 bus station [bʌs `steʃən]。

bus stop 公車站

stop 有「停止、靜止」的意思，因此公車停下來載客又出發，規模較小的公車站點，就稱為 bus stop [bʌs stɑp]。

underground 地下鐵

在英國，地下鐵不像美國一樣叫做 subway，而是稱為 underground [`ʌndɚˏgraʊnd]。under 是「在～下面」，ground 則是「地面」，因此可以簡單推得是指在地面之下的地下鐵。

stop 下車鈴

雖然公車的下車鈴系統會因為公車而有所不同，但一般只要按下寫著 STOP（停止）的按鍵就可以了。紐約公車的下車鈴，還有窗邊拉繩或膠條的形式，只要拉繩子或按壓膠條，公車前方的電子顯示板就會出現 STOP REQUESTED（要求下車）的燈號。

priority seat 博愛座

priority 是「優先權」，seat 則是「座位」，老人、孕婦及殘障人士等可以優先入座的博愛座，就稱為 priority seat [praɪˋɔrətɪ sit]。

platform 月台

火車站或地鐵站中，乘客上下車的月台叫做 platform [ˋplæt͵fɔrm]。根據目的地不同，對應的月台號碼也會不同，因此搭乘之前務必先確認過再上車。

exit 出口

從地下鐵要出站的時候，只要跟著 exit [ˋɛksɪt]（出口）或 way out [we aʊt]（出口方向）的標誌移動就可以了。另外，紐約的地下鐵出口並沒有標示號碼，而是直接寫著出去後會到達的地點。

生動的旅遊情報

交通方式面面觀

在國外旅行，
有時候可以見到
在自己國家看不到的交通工具。
一起來認識旅行時，
可以利用的
代表性交通工具有哪些吧！

Eurail Pass 歐洲火車通行票

也稱為「歐鐵聯票」，持有此票券，可以在一定期間內不限次數搭乘歐洲 28 個國家的國有鐵路。與飛機不同，搭火車不須登機手續和等待時間，可以自由穿越歐洲各國國境移動，非常方便，是在歐洲旅行的背包客經常利用的交通方式。

Greyhound 灰狗巴士

灰狗巴士成立超過一百年，是北美地區有名的長途巴士營運公司。雖然因為行經站點多，而較花時間，且座位也不舒服，但與火車或飛機相比，價錢便宜是優點。

Amtrack 美國國鐵

美國代表性的鐵路公司，是 America（美國）與 Track [træk]（火車軌道）的合成詞。它橫跨了廣闊的美國，連接 500 個以上的城市。依據列車的不同，有時候會有能睡覺的臥鋪車廂、能用餐的餐車車廂、販賣簡單零嘴的酒吧車廂。

yellow cab / black cab
黃色計程車／黑色計程車

計程車除了 taxi [`tæksɪ] 之外也可以稱為 cab。yellow cab [`jɛlo kæb] 是美國代表性的計程車公司，顏色是黃色（yellow）。駕駛座和後座之間裝設有防彈玻璃，只能坐後座。在有小費文化的美國，比車資多給 10～15% 左右的小費是很普遍的。另一方面，black cab [blæk kæb] 則是英國政府所營運的計程車，黑色（black）的外觀是較經典的設計。與台灣不同，駕駛座旁邊是放行李的地方，後座則是客人的座位。

tram 電車

如果說在地下有地下鐵，在地上則有稱為「電車」的 tram [træm]。在美國，像舊金山、費城、波士頓等都市，可以搭乘電車在市區移動。而在歐洲如德國、法國、捷克等地，也經常能看見這種交通工具。

在飯店

08 入住飯店

09 使用飯店設施、服務

10 解決飯店的問題

11 飯店退房

08 入住飯店

◎ 請聽以下對話，並跟著說說看。 08-1

對話A

服務人員 Hello. How can I help you?
[hə`lo] [haʊ kæn aɪ hɛlp ju]

秀智 **I'd like to** check in.
[aɪd laɪk tu tʃɛk ɪn]

對話B

服務人員 What kind of room would you like?
[hwɑt kaɪnd ɑv rum wʊd ju laɪk]

振洙 **I'd like a room with** a single bed.
[aɪd laɪk ə rum wɪð ə `sɪŋgəl bɛd]

句型 15 **I'd like to +** 動詞 **.** 我想要～。

I'd 是 I would 的縮寫，「would like to＋動詞」表示「想做～」，是「want to＋動詞」更客氣的說法。可以在 I'd like to 後面帶入像 order [`ɔrdɚ]「點餐」、change [tʃendʒ]「更改」、get [gɛt]「得到」等的動詞，就能在飯店、餐廳、商店等各種場所表明自己想要的東西。

句型 15 我想要辦理入住。

句型 16 我想要一間有一張單人床的房間。

08-1

抵達飯店後，必須先到櫃台辦理入住手續，再接受房間分配。一起來學學在這種時刻，可以怎麼告訴服務人員自己的需求吧！

對話 A

服務人員 哈囉，有什麼我能幫你的嗎？

秀智 我想要辦理入住。

對話 B

服務人員 你想要哪種房間？

振洙 我想要一間有一張單人床的房間。

新出現的單字

check in [tʃɛk ɪn] 辦理入住（手續）

kind [kaɪnd] 種類

room [rum] 房間

single [`sɪŋgəl] 單人的

bed [bɛd] 床

雖然 kind 作為形容詞是「親切的」的意思，不過作為名詞則是表示「種類」。

句型 16 I'd like a room with + 設施／景觀 .

我想要一間有～的房間。

「would like＋名詞」意思是「想要～」，因此 I'd like a room 表示「我想要一間房間」，後面加上「with＋設施／景觀」，就可以表示想要有該設施或景觀的房間。可以像 I'd like a room with a bathtub [`bæθ͵tʌb].（我想要有浴缸的房間）一樣表示想要的設施，也可以像 I'd like a room with a city view [`sɪtɪ vju].（我想要看得到市區景觀的房間）一樣表達想從房間窗戶看到的景觀。

句型15 練習

我想要～。

08-2

請將單字帶入空格內並說說看。 08-2

I'd like to ______.

我想要 ______ 。

order room service[1]
[ˋɔrdɚ rum ˋsɝvɪs]
叫客房服務

get laundry service
[gɛt ˋlɔndrɪ ˋsɝvɪs]
使用洗衣服務

change my room
[tʃendʒ maɪ rum]
換房間

make a reservation[2]
[mek ə ˏrɛzɚˋveʃən]
預訂

1 order room service order 是「點餐」的意思，room service 是指「客房服務」，即飯店直接將餐飲送至客房的服務，通常費用會比在餐廳用餐貴上 10~15% 左右。

2 make a reservation reservation 是「預訂（名詞）」的意思，要說「進行預訂」的時候，會搭配動詞 make（做），說成 make a reservation。另外，「取消（我的）預訂」則是 cancel my reservation。

句型16
練習

我想要一間有～的房間。

08-3

請將單字帶入空格內並說說看。 08-3

I'd like a room with ______.

我想要一間有 ______ 的房間。

a double bed
[ə `dʌbəl bɛd]
一張雙人床

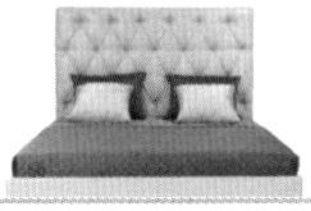

twin beds[1]
[twɪn bɛdz]
兩張單人床

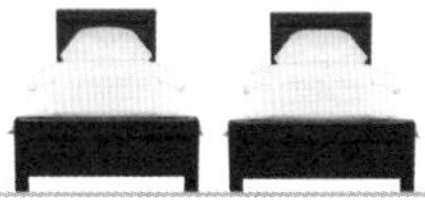

an ocean view[2]
[æn `oʃən vju]
海景

a balcony
[ə `bælkənɪ]
陽台

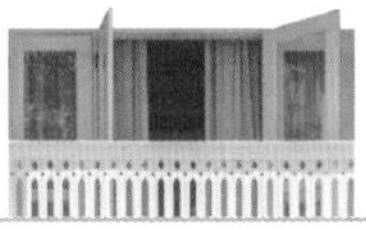

1 **twin beds** twin 是「雙胞胎的、一雙的」，twin beds 表示房裡有兩張像雙胞胎一樣的單人床。

2 **an ocean view** ocean 是「海洋」，view 則是「景觀」。a partial ocean view 表示部分海景，而 a garden view [ə `gɑrdən vju] 表示看得見庭園景觀，a city view [ə `sɪtɪ vju] 則表示市區景觀。

對話 終於進入了飯店

08-4

請聽以下對話，並跟著說說看。 08-4

進入飯店的秀智，為了辦理入住手續而前往櫃台。

秀智 Hello. **I'd like to check in.**
[hə`lo] [aɪd laɪk tu tʃɛk ɪn]

服務人員 Do you have a reservation?
[du ju hæv ə ˌrɛzɚ`veʃən]

秀智 No. Are there any rooms available?
[no] [ɑr ðɛr `ɛnɪ rumz ə`veləbəl]

available 可利用的

服務人員 Yes. What kind of room do you have in mind?
[jɛs] [hwɑt kaɪnd ɑv rum du ju hæv ɪn maɪnd]

秀智 **I'd like a room with a single bed.**
[aɪd laɪk ə rum wɪð ə `sɪŋgəl bɛd]

mind 心意、想法

服務人員 How long will you be staying?
[haʊ lɔŋ wɪl ju bi steɪŋ]

秀智 Two nights.
[tu naɪts]

服務人員 Okay. Here is your room key.
[ˌo`ke] [hɪr ɪz jʊɚ rum ki]

key 鑰匙

秀智 哈囉。**我想辦理入住。**
服務人員 你有預訂嗎？
秀智 沒有。有可以住的房間嗎？
服務人員 有的。你考慮要哪種房間？
秀智 **我想要一間有一張單人床的房間。**
服務人員 你會住多久呢？
秀智 兩個晚上。
服務人員 好的，這裡是你的房間鑰匙。

驗收 08 入住飯店

解答在 216 頁

A 請從選項中選出能填入空格的單字。

選項 **single** | **like** | **kind** | **with**

① 我想要辦理入住。

I'd ______ to check in.

② 你想要哪種房間？

What ______ of room would you like?

③ 我想要一間有一張單人床的房間。

I'd like a room ______ a ______ bed.

B 請在選項中找出適當的表達方式，並完成下列句子。

選項 **an ocean view** | **change my room** | **order room service** | **a double bed**

① 我想要換房間。

I'd like to ______.

② 我想要叫客房服務。

I'd like to ______.

③ 我想要有一張雙人床的房間。

I'd like a room with ______.

④ 我想要有海景的房間。

I'd like a room with ______.

09 使用飯店設施、服務

◎ 請聽以下對話，並跟著說說看。 09-1

對話A

振洙 **Where is the** restaurant?

[hwɛr ɪz ðə `rɛstərənt]

服務人員 It's located on the third floor.

[ɪts `loketɪd ɑn ðə θɝd flɔr]

對話B

秀智 **Is there** room service?

[ɪz ðɛr rum `sɝvɪs]

服務人員 Yes, we offer 24-hour room service.

[jɛs wi `ɔfɚ `twɛntɪˏfor aʊr rum `sɝvɪs]

句型 17 **Where is the + 地點 ?** ～在哪裡？

詢問自己找尋的地點在哪裡時，可以用 where（哪裡）這個字，簡單以 Where is the ~? 提問。這個句型不只能用來詢問飯店內設施的位置，也可用來詢問觀光景點或店家在哪裡。

句型 17 餐廳在哪裡？

句型 18 有客房服務嗎？

09-1

為了投宿客人的方便，飯店會提供各式各樣的服務及設施。請熟悉詢問是否有某設施與服務的表達方式，徹底地利用飯店吧！

對話 A

振洙 餐廳在哪裡？

服務人員 位在三樓。

對話 B

秀智 有客房服務嗎？

服務人員 有，我們提供 24 小時的客房服務。

新出現的單字

restaurant [`rɛstərənt] 餐廳

locate [lo`ket] 使位在、找出（位置）

third [θɝd] 第三的

floor [flor] 層

room service [rum `sɝvɪs] 客房服務（將餐點送到客房的服務）

offer [`ɔfɚ] 提供

hour [aʊr] 時間

句型 18 **Is there + 服務／設施 ?** 有～嗎？

因為「There is＋名詞」是「有～」的意思，改成疑問句「Is there＋名詞?」就變為「有～嗎？」的意思，後面可以帶入單數型態的名詞，以確認飯店有沒有某種服務或設施。在這個句型中，如果帶入的名詞是可數名詞的話，要在前面加 a 或 an，變成「Is there a [an]＋名詞?」，如 Is there a swimming pool?（有游泳池嗎？）。

句型17 練習

～在哪裡？

09-2

請將單字帶入空格內並說說看。 09-2

Where is the ______?

______ 在哪裡？

front desk
[frʌnt dɛsk]
櫃台、諮詢台

lobby
[\`lɑbɪ]
大廳

sauna
[\`saʊnə]
桑拿室

fitness center[1]
[\`fɪtnɪs \`sɛntɚ]
健身中心

convenience store
[kən\`vinjəns stɔr]
便利商店

swimming pool
[\`swɪmɪŋ pul]
游泳池

■ **多樣的飯店設施** 除了這些飯店設施，還有提供簡單餐飲的 cafeteria [ˌkæfə\`tɪrɪə]（自助式餐廳）、販賣酒精飲料的 bar [bɑr]（酒吧）、水療中心 spa [spɑ]、提供商務出差者電腦及列表機的 business center [\`bɪznɪs \`sɛntɚ] 等。

1 **fitness center** 有跑步機等運動器材的地方，fitness 是「健康」，center 則是「中心」的意思。

句型18 練習

有～嗎？

09-3

◎ 請將單字帶入空格內並說說看。 09-3

Is there ______?

有 ______ 嗎？

laundry service
[ˋlɔndrɪ ˋsɝvɪs]
洗衣服務

valet parking[1]
[ˋvælɪt ˋpɑrkɪŋ]
代客泊車、代客停車

a wake-up call service[2]
[ə wek ʌp kɔl ˋsɝvɪs]
晨喚服務

free WiFi
[fri ˋwaɪˏfaɪ]
免費無線網路

1 valet parking valet 是「停車員」，parking 則是「停車」。客人的車子抵達後，服務人員代替客人將車停進專用停車場的服務，就稱為 valet parking。

2 a wake-up call service 「晨喚」是指飯店配合指定時間打電話通知客人的服務，正確的英文說法是 wake-up call，而非我們一般習慣說的 morning call。wake-up 是「叫醒」，call 則是「電話」。

對話 吃飯皇帝大

09-4

◎ 請聽以下對話，並跟著說說看。 09-4

正在煩惱早餐該如何解決的振洙，決定試著向服務人員問問看。

振洙 **Is there room service?**
[ɪz ðɛr rum `sɝvɪs]

服務人員 No, but there is a good restaurant for breakfast.
[no bʌt ðɛr ɪz ə gʊd `rɛstərənt fɔr `brɛkfəst]

振洙 **Where is the restaurant?**
[hwɛr ɪz ðə `rɛstərənt]

breakfast 早餐

服務人員 It is at the end of the lobby.
[ɪt ɪz æt ði ɛnd ɑv ðə `lɑbɪ]

end 盡頭

振洙 What time can I have breakfast?
[hwɑt taɪm kæn aɪ hæv `brɛkfəst]

服務人員 Breakfast is served from 7 to 9 a.m.
[`brɛkfəst ɪz sɝvd frɑm `sɛvən tu naɪn e ɛm]

serve 提供（餐飲）

振洙 Is it a buffet?
[ɪz ɪt ə bʌ`fe]

buffet 自助餐

服務人員 Yes, it is.
[jɛs ɪt ɪz]

振洙 **有客房服務嗎？**
服務人員 沒有，不過有可以用早餐的好餐廳。
振洙 **餐廳在哪裡？**
服務人員 在大廳的盡頭。
振洙 我幾點可以吃早餐呢？
服務人員 早餐從早上 7 點供應到 9 點。
振洙 是自助餐嗎？
服務人員 是的，沒錯。

驗收 09 使用飯店設施、服務

解答在 217 頁

A 請從選項中選出能填入空格的單字。

選項 **restaurant** | **floor** | **room** | **where**

① 餐廳在哪裡？

______ is the ______?

② 位在三樓。

It's located on the third ______.

③ 有客房服務嗎？

Is there ______ service?

B 請在選項中找出適當的表達方式，並完成下列句子。

選項 **convenience store** | **free WiFi** | **laundry service** | **swimming pool**

① 便利商店在哪裡？

Where is the ______?

② 游泳池在哪裡？

Where is the ______?

③ 有免費無線網路嗎？

Is there ______?

④ 有洗衣服務嗎？

Is there ______?

10 解決飯店的問題

◎ 請聽以下對話，並跟著說說看。 10-1

對話A

振洙 **The** air conditioner **doesn't work.**
[ði ɛr kən`dɪʃənɚ `dʌzənt wɝk]

服務人員 Oh, I'm sorry for any inconvenience.
[o aɪm `sɑrɪ fɔr `ɛnɪ ˏɪnkən`vinjəns]

對話B

服務人員 Front desk. How can I help you?
[frʌnt dɛsk] [haʊ kæn aɪ hɛlp ju]

秀智 **There is no** toilet paper.
[ðɛr ɪz no `tɔɪlɪt `pepɚ]

句型 19 **The** 物品 **+ doesn't work.** ～故障了。

work 是「（機器）運作」，doesn't work 則是「不運作」，也就是「故障」的意思。當飯店房內的空調、電燈、電視等物品無法開啟時，請試著用這個句型向櫃台員工反應。另外，如果想要強調物品現在沒在運作的狀態，也可以說「The 物品＋is not working.」。

句型 19 空調故障了。

句型 20 沒有衛生紙。

10-1

住在飯店裡，有時候會發生意想不到的問題。來看看向飯店員工說明房內有什麼問題時，所使用的句型吧！

對話 A

振洙　空調故障了。

服務人員　噢，造成你的任何不便，我很抱歉。

對話 B

服務人員　櫃台你好，有什麼我能幫你的嗎？

秀智　沒有衛生紙。

新出現的單字

air conditioner [ɛr kən`dɪʃənɚ] 空調

work [wɝk]（機器）運作

inconvenience [ˌɪnkən`vinjəns] 不便

toilet paper [`tɔɪlɪt `pepɚ]（捲筒式）廁所用衛生紙

句型 20 There is no + 物品 . 沒有～。

「There is＋名詞.」是「有～」的意思，若要表示「沒有～」，只要在名詞前面加入 no，形成「There is no＋名詞 .」就可以了。雖然「There is not [isn't]＋名詞.」也有相同的意思，不過 no 寫在名詞前面，更有強調物品沒有了的意味。但請別忘了，這時接在後面的名詞一定要使用單數型態。

句型19 練習

～故障了。

10-2

◎ 請將單字帶入空格內並說說看。 10-2

The ______ doesn't work.

______ 故障了。

heater
[`hitɚ]
暖氣

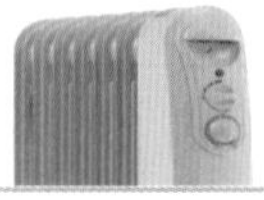

shower
[`ʃaʊɚ]
淋浴器、淋浴間

remote control[1]
[rɪ`mot kən`trol]
遙控器

lamp
[læmp]
檯燈

telephone
[`tɛlə͵fon]
電話

fridge[2]
[frɪdʒ]
冰箱

1 **remote control** remote 是「遠距的、距離遙遠的」，control 則是「控制裝置、控制」，合在一起就是指可以遠距控制的「遙控器」了。

2 **fridge** 冰箱也稱為 refrigerator [rɪ`frɪdʒə͵retɚ]。根據飯店的不同，有些飯店也會在冰箱內準備好礦泉水或啤酒等飲料。若喝了這些飲料，通常在退房結帳時，需要支付費用。

句型20 練習

沒有～。

10-3

請將單字帶入空格內並說說看。 10-3

There is no ______.

沒有 ______ 。

towel
[`taʊəl]
毛巾

shampoo
[ʃæm`pu]
洗髮乳

soap
[sop]
肥皂

toothbrush
[`tuθˌbrʌʃ]
牙刷

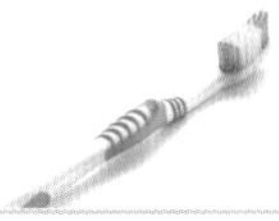

hairdryer
[`hɛrˌdraɪɚ]
吹風機

razor
[`rezɚ]
刮鬍刀

■ **飯店內的各種免費用品** 飯店所提供的盥洗用品、化妝品、拖鞋、浴袍等免費生活用品稱為 amenity [ə`minətɪ]。除了上面提到的物品外，也會提供 shower gel [`ʃaʊɚ dʒɛl]（沐浴乳）、conditioner [kən`dɪʃənɚ]（潤髮乳）、shower cap [`ʃaʊɚ kæp]（浴帽）、comb [kom]（梳子）、toothpaste [`tuθˌpest]（牙膏）等各種用品。

對話 狀況百出的飯店

10-4

◎ 請聽以下對話，並跟著說說看。 10-4

辦理入住後進到住房，房裡卻是一團亂。為了客訴，秀智拿起了電話。

服務人員 Good evening, front desk.
[gʊd `ivnɪŋ frʌnt dɛsk]

秀智 Hello. This is Room 104.
[hə`lo] [ðɪs ɪz rum wʌn o for]

服務人員 Yes, ma'am. How can I help you?
[jɛs mæm] [haʊ kæn aɪ hɛlp ju]

ma'am 女士

秀智 **The air conditioner doesn't work.**
[ði ɛr kən`dɪʃənɚ `dʌzənt wɝk]

服務人員 I'm sorry. I'll send someone to check it.
[aɪm `sɑrɪ ] [ aɪl sɛnd `sʌm͵wʌn tu tʃɛk ɪt]

check 確認

秀智 Also, **there is no toilet paper.**
[`ɔlso ðɛr ɪz no `tɔɪlɪt `pepɚ]

Can I move to another room?
[kæn aɪ muv tu ə`nʌðɚ rum]

move 移動

服務人員 Just a moment. Let me check for you.
[dʒʌst ə `moment] [lɛt mi tʃɛk fɔr ju]

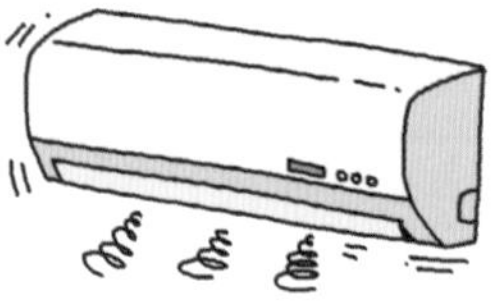

服務人員 晚安，櫃台你好。
秀智 哈囉，這裡是 104 號房。
服務人員 是的女士，有什麼我能幫你的嗎？
秀智 **空調故障了。**
服務人員 很抱歉，我將派人去看看。
秀智 然後也**沒有衛生紙了**。我可以換到其他房間嗎？
服務人員 請稍等，我為你確認一下。

驗收 10 解決飯店的問題

解答在 217 頁

A 請從選項中選出能填入空格的單字。

選項 **work** | **sorry** | **paper** | **conditioner**

① 空調故障了。

The air ______ doesn't ______.

② 沒有衛生紙。

There is no toilet ______.

③ 噢，造成你的任何不便，我很抱歉。

Oh, I'm ______ for any inconvenience.

B 請在選項中找出適當的表達方式，並完成下列句子。

選項 **heater** | **razor** | **towel** | **telephone**

① 電話故障了。

The ______ doesn't work.

② 暖氣故障了。

The ______ doesn't work.

③ 沒有毛巾。

There is no ______.

④ 沒有刮鬍刀。

There is no ______.

11 飯店退房

◎ 請聽以下對話，並跟著說說看。 11-1

對話A

服務人員 **I'm sorry for** the error.
[aɪm `sɑrɪ fɔr ði `ɛrɚ]

振洙 That's okay.
[ðæts ˏo`ke]

對話B

服務人員 How would you like to pay?
[haʊ wʊd ju laɪk tu pe]

秀智 **Is it possible to** pay by credit card?
[ɪz ɪt `pɑsəbəl tu pe baɪ `krɛdɪt kɑrd]

句型 21 I'm sorry for + 做錯的事 . 對於～，我很抱歉。

道歉時，通常最常使用的是表示「對不起」的 I'm sorry.。特別為某件事情道歉時，後面只要加上「for＋做錯的事」來表達就可以了。這時，介系詞 for 後面「做錯的事」的部分，可以加上名詞或動名詞：名詞能用像 error（失誤）一樣表示抽象概念的字，或是人物、事物的名稱；動名詞則是指動詞加上 ing 的型態，如動詞 call [kɔl]（打電話）的動名詞是 calling [`kɔlɪŋ]。

句型 21 **對於這個錯誤，我很抱歉。**

句型 22 **可以用信用卡結帳嗎？**

11-1

在飯店的最後一天，要退房、結算並且支付費用。來學習道歉時所使用的句型，以及與退房相關好用的表達方式吧！

對話A

服務人員　對於這個錯誤，我很抱歉。

振洙　沒有關係。

對話B

服務人員　你想要怎麼結帳？

秀智　可以用信用卡結帳嗎？

新出現的單字

sorry [ˋsɑrɪ] 抱歉的、遺憾的

error [ˋɛrɚ] 失誤、錯誤

okay [ˌoˈke] 沒關係的

pay [pe] 支付（金額）

possible [ˋpɑsəbəl] 可能的

credit card [ˋkrɛdɪt kɑrd] 信用卡

句型 22 Is it possible to + 動詞 ? 可以～嗎？

possible 是「可能的、可以的」的意思。想詢問某個行動是否可行時，能使用「Is it possible to＋動詞？」這個句型。這時對可行的事情可以回答 Yes, it is. / Yes, you can.，而對不可行的事情則可以回答 No, it isn't. / No, you can't.。

句型21 練習

對於～，我很抱歉。

11-2

◎ 請將單字帶入空格內並說說看。 11-2

I'm sorry for ______.

對於 ______ ，我很抱歉。

the mistake
[ðə mɪ`stek]
失誤

the delay
[ðə dɪ`le]
延遲、耽誤

calling so early[1]
[`kɔlɪŋ so `ɝlɪ]
這麼早打電話來

being late[2]
[`biɪŋ let]
遲到

1 calling so early call 是「打電話」，so 是「如此地、這麼地」，early 則是「早」。動詞 call 加上 ing，形成動名詞 calling，就成了「打電話（這件事）」的意思。相反地，「這麼晚打電話（這件事）」就是 calling so late [`kɔlɪŋ so let]。

2 being late be late 是「晚了、遲到」的意思，因為 for 後面要加上「動詞＋ing」，所以 be 要加上 ing，變成 being。

句型22 練習

可以～嗎？

11-3

請將單字帶入空格內並說說看。 11-3

Is it possible to ______?

可以 ______ 嗎？

check out late

[tʃɛk aʊt let]

晚點退房

leave my luggage here[1]

[liv maɪ `lʌgɪdʒ hɪr]

把我的行李寄放在這裡

stay one more night

[ste wʌn mor naɪt]

多住一晚

leave a day earlier[2]

[liv ə de `ɝlɪr]

早一天離開

1 leave my luggage here 這是在入住之前或退房之後，詢問是否能將行李寄放在飯店時，可以使用的表達方式。leave 有「（將物品）託（給某人）」的意思。

2 leave a day earlier 動詞 leave 除了有「寄、託」的意思之外，也有「離開（地點）、出發」的意思。另外 earlier 是 early 的比較級，表示「較早」。

對話 退房時要看仔細

11-4

◎ 請聽以下對話，並跟著說說看。 11-4

住飯店的最後一天，秀智為了辦理退房而來到櫃檯。

秀智 I'd like to check out. Room 104.

[aɪd laɪk tu tʃɛk aʊt] [rum wʌn o for]

服務人員 Here is your bill.

[hɪr ɪz jʊə bɪl]

秀智 What is this extra 20 dollars for?

[hwɑt ɪz ðɪs `ɛkstrə `twɛntɪ `dɑlə·z fɔr]

extra 額外的

服務人員 It's for laundry service.

[ɪts fɔr `lɔndrɪ `sɝvɪs]

秀智 But I didn't use it.

[bʌt aɪ `dɪdənt juz ɪt]

服務人員 Oh, **I'm sorry for the error.**

[o aɪm `sɑrɪ fɔr ði `ɛrə]

Here is your correct bill.

[hɪr ɪz jʊə kə`rɛkt bɪl]

秀智 Thanks. **Is it possible to pay by credit card?**

[θæŋks] [ɪz ɪt `pɑsəbəl tu pe baɪ `krɛdɪt kɑrd]

服務人員 Certainly.

[`sɝtənlɪ]

秀智	我想辦理退房，是 104 號房。
服務人員	這裡是你的帳單。
秀智	這額外的 20 美金是什麼（費用）？
服務人員	是洗衣服務（的費用）。
秀智	但是我並沒有使用這項服務。
服務人員	噢，**對於這個錯誤，我很抱歉**。這裡是你正確的帳單。
秀智	謝了。**可以用信用卡結帳嗎？**
服務人員	當然。

驗收 11 飯店退房

解答在 218 頁

A 請從選項中選出能填入空格的單字。

選項 **credit** | **error** | **possible** | **pay**

① 你想要怎麼結帳？

How would you like to ______?

② 可以用信用卡結帳嗎？

Is it ______ to pay by ______ card?

③ 對於這個錯誤，我很抱歉。

I'm sorry for the ______.

B 請在選項中找出適當的表達方式，並完成下列句子。

選項 **leave my luggage here** | **the delay** | **calling so early** | **check out late**

① 對於這個延遲，我很抱歉。

I'm sorry for ______.

② 對於這麼早打電話來，我很抱歉。

I'm sorry for ______.

③ 可以晚點退房嗎？

Is it possible to ______?

④ 可以把我的行李寄放在這裡嗎？

Is it possible to ______?

11-5

Vacancy 空房

vacancy [`vekənsɪ] 是「空位」的意思。規模小的飯店，會在飯店外掛上標誌來表示有沒有空房間，Vacancy 表示有空房間，No Vacancy 則表示沒有空房間，有時也會使用複數型 Vacancies 表示。

Reception 飯店櫃檯

飯店的櫃台在英國或歐洲會標示為 reception [rɪ`sɛpʃən]。在這裡可以辦理入住或退房，也可以得到和飯店相關的所有幫助。同時，這也是在公司或公共機關的接待處會看得到的單字。

Concierge 禮賓服務台

在頂級飯店裡，前台兩側有 concierge [ˌkɑnsɪ`ɛrʒ]，也就是提供客人所有需要的服務的地方。除了提供交通、觀光、美食等各種資訊外，也會幫忙訂購不容易買到的表演門票。

Complimentary water 免費飲水

complimentary [ˌkɑmplə`mɛntərɪ] 意為「免費的」。如果在飯店提供的物品上看見這個標示，就表示是免費的，可以輕鬆地享受了。許多飯店會免費提供礦泉水一瓶、即溶咖啡和茶包。

Do not disturb 請勿打擾

disturb [dɪs`tɝb] 是表示「妨礙」的動詞。在飯店房間門把掛上表示「請勿打擾」的 Do not disturb 掛牌的話，就可以限制飯店員工進入房間。如果不需要客房打掃或想安靜休息，就請掛上這個吊牌吧。

Please make up room 請整理房間

make up [mek ʌp] 應該以「化妝」的意思較為大眾所知，但 make up room 是「清掃房間、整理房間」的意思。在飯店房間門把掛上 Please make up room 掛牌的話，就表示請人清掃房間。

Minibar 迷你吧

意指飯店客房中的小型冰箱。mini [`mɪnɪ] 是「迷你的」，bar [bɑr] 則是「（酒類、簡單食物的）販售台」的意思。迷你吧裡面備有各種飲料和零食，吃了的話，在退房時就會被要求付費，不過在高級渡假村裡，這屬於住客服務的一部分，因此有時也會免費提供。

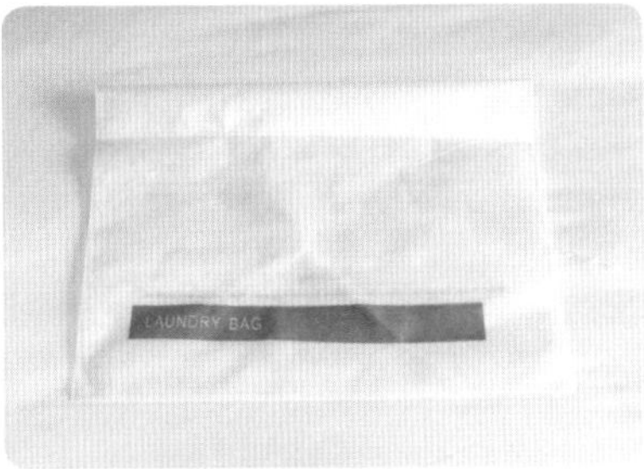

Laundry bag 洗衣袋

想利用飯店所提供的洗衣服務的話，只要將送洗的衣物放進在衣櫃中的 laundry bag [`lɔndrɪ bæg] 後，再交給飯店就可以了。雖然比一般的洗衣費用還高，但是會把衣服烘乾才送回來，所以相當便利。

生動的旅遊情報

多樣的飯店客房

依據價格與住宿需求不同，
飯店客房的種類
可以說是千變萬化。
來認識預訂飯店時，
一定要知道的客房種類吧！

single room 單人房

有一張單人床（single bed）的一人用客房，是為獨自入住的旅客準備的房間。

double room 雙人房

有一張雙人床（double bed）的兩人用客房，主要是愛侶們會使用的客房。

twin room 雙床雙人房

有兩張單人床（single bed）的兩人用客房，因為床鋪是分開的，很適合與朋友一起住。

triple room 三人房

triple [`trɪpəl] 表示「三個的」，所以 triple room 是可供三人使用的房間，基本上會提供一張雙人床（double bed），外加一張摺疊式床鋪。

suite 套房

一般來說是指除了附有浴室的寢室之外，還有一個額外隔出來的客廳兼招待室，是比一般客房更貴又更高級的房型。雖然我們下意識會想說出「suite room」，不過在英文裡要去掉 room，只說 suite [swit]。和意為「甜蜜的」的 sweet [swit] 發音相同，請別搞混了。

smoking room 吸菸房

non-smoking room 禁菸房

在飯店客房中，有分可以吸菸的 smoking room [`smokɪŋ rum]，和不可以吸菸的 non-smoking room [ˌnɑn`smokɪŋ rum]。因為吸菸房會有香菸的味道，可能會讓不吸菸者感到不快，訂房時最好避開。

dormitory room 宿舍房

這是在廉價的旅社或青年旅館裡很常見到的房間型態。dormitory [`dɔrməˌtorɪ] 是「宿舍」的意思，dormitory room 則像宿舍一樣，一間房裡有好幾張上下鋪，廁所和廚房設施大多需要多人共同使用。

在餐廳

12 預訂餐廳

13 點餐

14 對餐廳的不滿之處

15 速食餐廳

16 咖啡廳

12 預訂餐廳

請聽以下對話，並跟著說說看。 12-1

對話A

振洙 **I'd like to book a table for** tonight.
[aɪd laɪk tu bʊk ə `tebəl fɔr tə`naɪt]

服務生 I'm sorry, but we are fully booked.
[aɪm `sɑrɪ bʌt wi ɑr `fʊlɪ bʊkt]

對話B

秀智 **Could we have a table**
[kʊd wi hæv ə `tebəl

by the window?
baɪ ðə `wɪndo]

服務生 Of course.
[ɑv kors]

句型 23 I'd like to book a table for + 時間 .

我想預訂～的位子。

如同前面學過，「I'd like to＋動詞」是表示「想要做～」。book 除了有「書」的意思外，當動詞時則表示「預訂」。因此 book a table 就變成了「預訂（餐廳）座位」的意思。在後面加上「for＋時間／星期幾／日期」的話，就可以表達具體想要預訂的時間了。

句型 23 我想預訂今天晚上的位子。

句型 24 我們可以坐窗邊的座位嗎？

12-1

想在很受歡迎的餐廳裡用餐的話，最好提早預訂。來學在預訂餐廳時用的表達方式吧！

對話 A

振洙 我想預訂今天晚上的位子。

服務生 不好意思，我們都訂滿了。

對話 B

秀智 我們可以坐窗邊的座位嗎？

服務生 當然可以。

新出現的單字

book [bʊk] 預約

table [`tebəl] 餐桌、桌子

tonight [tə`naɪt] 今晚

fully [`fʊlɪ] 完全地

by [baɪ] ～旁邊

window [`wɪndo] 窗戶

句型 24 Could we have a table + 想要的座位 ?

我們可以坐～的座位嗎？

「Could we＋動詞？」是比「Can we＋動詞？」更客氣的表達方式，為一有禮貌地詢問「我們可以～嗎？」的句型。Could we have a table ~ ? 直譯的話是「我們可以有～的桌子嗎？」的意思。若後面加上修飾 a table 的字詞（如人數、座位位置等），就變成了「可以坐～的座位嗎？」的意思。

句型23 練習

我想預訂～的位子。

12-2

請將單字帶入空格內並說說看。 12-2

I’d like to book a table for ______.

我想預訂 ______ 的位子。

11 a.m.[1]
[ɪ`lɛvən e ɛm]
上午 11 點

7 p.m.[1]
[`sɛvən pi ɛm]
晚上 7 點

6 o’clock
[sɪks ə`klɑk]
6 點整

tomorrow night
[tə`mɔro naɪt]
明天晚上

Sunday lunch
[`sʌnde lʌntʃ]
星期日午餐

this Friday[2]
[ðɪs `fraɪ͵de]
這個星期五

1 **11 a.m. / 7 p.m.** a.m.（上午）與 p.m.（下午）是拉丁文 ante meridiem 與 post meridiem 的縮寫。meridiem 是「正中午」，ante 是「～之前」，post 是「～之後」的意思，因此 a.m. 就成為「正午前（＝上午）」、p.m. 是「正午後（＝下午）」。

2 **this Friday** 「this＋星期～」是「這個星期～」的意思。此外，要說「下個星期～」的話，只要說「next＋星期～」就可以了，例如「下個星期五」就是 next Friday。

句型24 練習　我們可以坐～的座位嗎？

12-3

請將單字帶入空格內並說說看。 12-3

Could we have a table ______?

我們可以坐 ______ 的座位嗎？

for two

[fɔr tu]

兩人座

on the terrace

[ɑn ðə ˋtɛrəs]

在露臺

in the non-smoking area[1]

[ɪn ðə nɑn ˋsmokɪŋˋɛrɪə]

在禁菸區

in the corner

[ɪn ðə ˋkɔrnɚ]

在角落

1 in the non-smoking area smoking（吸菸）前面加上表示「不、非」意思的 non 變成 non-smoking，就能表示「禁菸的」。因此 non-smoking area 是「禁菸區域」，也就是指在餐廳內的「禁菸區」。另外，「吸菸區」則是 smoking area。

對話 用餐時一定要預訂

12-4

◎ 請聽以下對話，並跟著說說看。 12-4

為了預訂以美食聞名的餐廳，秀智打了電話。

服務生 How can I help you?
[haʊ kæn aɪ hɛlp ju]

秀智 **I'd like to book a table for tonight.**
[aɪd laɪk tu bʊk ə `tebəl fɔr tə`naɪt]

服務生 For what time?
[fɔr hwɑt taɪm]

秀智 Seven o'clock.
[`sɛvən ə`klɑk]

服務生 How many in your party?
[haʊ `mɛnɪ ɪn jʊɚ `pɑrtɪ]

party 一行人、團體

秀智 Two. **Could we have a table by the window?**
[tu] [kʊd wi hæv ə `tebəl baɪ ðə `wɪndo]

服務生 No problem. May I have your name?
[no `prɑbləm] [me aɪ hæv jʊɚ nem]

秀智 My name is Susie Park.
[maɪ nem ɪz `suzi pɑrk]

服務生 有什麼我能幫你的嗎？
秀智 **我想預訂今天晚上的位子。**
服務生 幾點？
秀智 七點整。
服務生 你們幾位？
秀智 兩位。**我們可以坐窗邊的座位嗎？**
服務生 沒問題。能請你告訴我你的名字嗎？
秀智 我的名字是朴秀智。

驗收 12 預訂餐廳

解答在 218 頁

A 請從選項中選出能填入空格的單字。

選項 could | book | fully | window

① 我想預訂今天晚上的位子。

I'd like to ______ a table for tonight.

② 不好意思，我們都訂滿了。

I'm sorry, but we are ______ booked.

③ 我們可以坐窗邊的座位嗎？

______ we have a table by the ______?

B 請在選項中找出適當的表達方式，並完成下列句子。

選項 tomorrow night | in the corner | this Friday | for two

① 我想預訂這個星期五的位子。

I'd like to book a table for ______.

② 我想預訂明天晚上的位子。

I'd like to book a table for ______.

③ 我們可以坐兩人座的座位嗎？

Could we have a table ______?

④ 我們可以坐在角落的座位嗎？

Could we have a table ______?

13 點餐

◎ 請聽以下對話，並跟著說說看。 13-1

對話 A

振洙 **Does it come with** a salad?
[dʌz ɪt kʌm wɪð ə `sæləd]

服務生 Yes, it does.
[jɛs ɪt dʌz]

對話 B

秀智 **What do you recommend for** a main dish?
[hwɑt du ju ˌrɛkə`mɛnd fɔr ə men dɪʃ]

服務生 The fish and chips are very good here.
[ðə fɪʃ ænd tʃɪps ɑr `vɛrɪ gʊd hɪr]

句型 25 **Does it come with + 食物 ?** 這個有附～嗎？

with 是「與～一起」，come with 是「（一起）附上」的意思。就像在韓國餐廳點餐時會附贈小菜一樣，其他國家的餐點也會因為種類不同，而附有沙拉（salad）、麵包（bread）和薯條（fries [fraɪz]）等。只要 Does it come with 後面帶入食物名稱，就可以詢問是否附有這個食物。

句型 25 這個有附沙拉嗎？

句型 26 你推薦什麼作為主餐？

13-1

到餐廳裡要用英語向服務生點餐時，總是直冒冷汗，對吧？一起來學學去餐廳點餐時所使用的句型吧！

對話A

振洙　這個有附沙拉嗎？

服務生　是的，有附。

對話B

秀智　你推薦什麼作為主餐？

服務生　這裡的炸魚薯條非常美味。

新出現的單字

come with [kʌm wɪð] 附上～

salad [ˋsæləd] 沙拉

recommend [ˏrɛkəˋmɛnd] 推薦

main dish [men dɪʃ] 主餐

fish [fɪʃ] 魚

chips [tʃɪps] 炸薯條、薯片

fish and chips 是在裹麵衣油炸的白色魚肉旁，附上薯條的英國傳統料理。

句型 26 What do you recommend for + 菜色 ?

你推薦什麼作為～？

recommend 是「推薦」的意思，如果很難決定要點什麼時，可以用 What do you recommend?（你推薦什麼？）來詢問服務生的意見。這時，只要在後面加入「for＋菜色」來請服務生推薦作為主菜（main dish）、點心（dessert [dɪˋzɝt]）、飲料（drink [drɪŋk]）等的特定食物就可以了。

句型25 練習

這個有附～嗎？

13-2

◎ 請將單字帶入空格內並說說看。 13-2

Does it come with ______?

這個有附 ______ 嗎？

a drink
[ə drɪŋk]
飲料

rice
[raɪs]
白飯

soup
[sup]
湯

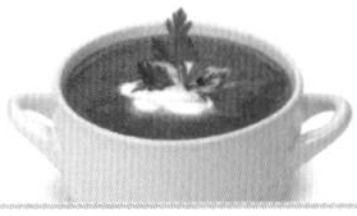

bread
[brɛd]
麵包

pickles[1]
[`pɪkəlz]
醃黃瓜

vegetables
[`vɛdʒətəbəlz]
蔬菜

■ **多樣的副餐** 在西方國家，很多時候餐點會附上馬鈴薯。他們很常吃像 fries [fraɪz]「炸薯條」、 mashed potato [mæʃt pə`teto]「馬鈴薯泥」、baked potato [bekt pə`teto]「烤馬鈴薯」等各式各樣的馬鈴薯料理。

1 pickles 是指用醋或鹽水浸泡醃製的黃瓜或蔬菜醃漬物。

句型26 練習

你推薦什麼作為～？

13-3

◎ 請將單字帶入空格內並說說看。 13-3

What do you recommend for ____?

你推薦什麼作為 ____？

an appetizer[1]
[æn ˋæpəˏtaɪzɚ]
前菜、開胃菜

a side dish
[ə saɪd dɪʃ]
附餐

dessert
[dɪˋzɝt]
點心、甜點

dressing
[ˋdrɛsɪŋ]
醬汁

wine
[waɪn]
葡萄酒

a fish dish[2]
[ə fɪʃ dɪʃ]
魚肉料理

1 an appetizer 開胃菜是指在用餐前為了提振食慾而吃的，如沙拉一類的簡單料理。在英國也叫作 starter [ˋstɑrtɚ]，有「開始的料理」的意思。

2 a fish dish dish 除了是「餐盤」的意思之外，也有「料理」的意思。因此 fish dish 就成了「魚肉料理」的意思。另外「肉類料理」是 meat dish [mit dɪʃ]，「海鮮料理」則是稱為 seafood dish [ˋsiˏfud dɪʃ]。

對話 點美味的食物

13-4

請聽以下對話，並跟著說說看。 13-4

到了餐廳的秀智，正看著滿是英文的菜單苦惱時，服務生就過來了。

服務生 Are you ready to order?
[ɑr ju ˋrɛdɪ tu ˋɔrdɚ]

秀智 **What do you recommend for a main dish?**
[hwɑt du ju ˏrɛkəˋmɛnd fɔr ə men dɪʃ]

服務生 The T-bone steak here is very good. **bone** 骨頭
[ðə ti bon stek hɪr ɪz ˋvɛrɪ gʊd]

秀智 **Does it come with a salad?**
[dʌz ɪt kʌm wɪð ə ˋsæləd]

服務生 Yes. It also comes with fries. **fries** 炸薯條
[jɛs] [ɪt ˋɔlso kʌmz wɪð fraɪz]

秀智 Sounds good. One T-bone steak, please.
[saʊndz gʊd] [wʌn ti bon stek pliz]

服務生 How would you like your steak?
[haʊ wʊd ju laɪk jʊɚ stek]

秀智 Well-done, please. **well-done** 全熟
[ˏwɛlˋdʌn pliz]

服務生 你準備好要點餐了嗎？
秀智 **你推薦什麼作為主餐？**
服務生 這裡的丁骨牛排（有 T 字型骨頭的牛排）非常美味。
秀智 **這個有附沙拉嗎？**
服務生 有的。也有附炸薯條。
秀智 聽起來不錯。（請給我）一個丁骨牛排，謝謝。
服務生 你的牛排要幾分熟呢？
秀智 （請給我）全熟，謝謝。

驗收 13 點餐

解答在 218 頁

A 請從選項中選出能填入空格的單字。

選項 **fish** **dish** **come** **recommend**

① 這個有附沙拉嗎？

Does it ______ with a salad?

② 你推薦什麼作為主餐？

What do you ______ for a main ______?

③ 這裡的炸魚薯條非常美味。

The ______ and chips are very good here.

B 請在選項中找出適當的表達方式，並完成下列句子。

選項 **dressing** **rice** **bread** **dessert**

① 這個有附麵包嗎？

Does it come with ______?

② 這個有附白飯嗎？

Does it come with ______?

③ 你推薦什麼作為甜點？

What do you recommend for ______?

④ 你推薦什麼作為醬汁（哪種醬汁）？

What do you recommend for ______?

14 對餐廳的不滿之處

請聽以下對話，並跟著說說看。 14-1

對話A

秀智 **This is too** salty.

[ðɪs ɪz tu `sɔltɪ]

服務生 I'm sorry. I will get you another one.

[aɪm `sɑrɪ ] [ aɪ wɪl gɛt ju ə`nʌðɚ wʌn]

對話B

振洙 Excuse me, but **I didn't order** a salad.

[ɪk`skjuz mi bʌt aɪ `dɪdənt `ɔrdɚ ə `sæləd]

服務生 I'm sorry. I'll bring you what you odered.

[aɪm `sɑrɪ ] [ aɪl brɪŋ ju hwɑt ju `ɔrdɚd]

句型 27 **This is too + 味道／狀態.** 這個太～了。

這是在餐廳裡對餐點的味道或狀態不滿意時，可以指著該菜餚使用的表達方式。如同 Me, too.（我也是）中所見的，too 雖然也很常被當作「也、還」的意義來用，但是也會用來表示「太過於」。與語意中性的 very（非常）不同，too 表示的是負面的「太過度」。

句型 27 這個太鹹了。

句型 28 我沒有點沙拉。

在餐廳用餐，總會有食物或帳單發生問題的時候，來學在這種時候要如何用英語理直氣壯地表達自己的不滿吧！

對話A

秀智　這個太鹹了。

服務生　很抱歉，我拿另一份給你（我為你換一份）。

對話B

振洙　不好意思，我沒有點沙拉。

服務生　很抱歉，我會把你點的餐點拿給你。

新出現的單字

salty [ˋsɔltɪ] 鹹的

another [əˋnʌðɚ] 另外的

bring [brɪŋ] 帶來

order [ˋɔrdɚ] 點餐

salt 是「鹽」，後面加上了 y，變成形容詞 salty 就是「有鹽的、鹹的」。

句型 28 I didn't order + 食物 . 我沒有點～。

order 表示「點餐」，前面加上否定的過去式助動詞 didn't，就是「沒有點餐」的意思。這是在服務生上錯食物，或者帳單上寫著自己沒有點的食物時，可以使用的句型。如果是上錯食物的情況，也可以簡單地指著餐點說 I didn't order this.（我沒有點這個）。

句型27
練習

這個太～了。

14-2

◎ 請將單字帶入空格內並說說看。 14-2

This is too ______.

這個太 ______ 了。

spicy[1]
[ˋspaɪsɪ]
辣的

sour
[ˋsaʊr]
酸的

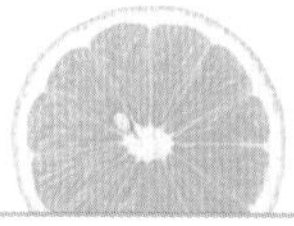

cold
[kold]
涼的、冷的

tough
[tʌf]
（肉）韌的

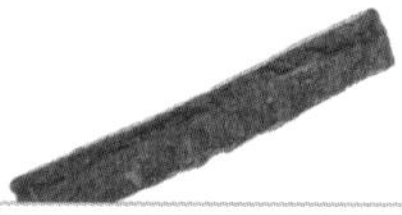

pink[2]
[pɪŋk]
（肉）太生的

bitter
[ˋbɪtɚ]
苦的

1 spicy spice [spaɪs] 是表示「辛香料」的名詞，形容詞 spicy 則表示「加辛香料的、以辛香料調味的」，因此放入許多辛香料就表示「辣的」。另外，表示「燙的、熱的」的 hot [hɑt] 也有「辣的」的意思。

2 pink pink 原本的意思是「粉紅色」，但因為肉不夠熟的時候，裡頭會是粉紅色的，所以也被用來表示「肉不夠熟的」。

句型28 練習

我沒有點～。

14-3

請將單字帶入空格內並說說看。 14-3

I didn’t order ________.

我沒有點 ________。

spaghetti[1]
[spə`gɛtɪ]
義大利麵

tomato soup
[tə`meto sup]
番茄湯

a steak
[ə stek]
牛排

roast beef
[rost bif]
烤牛肉

ice cream
[aɪs krim]
冰淇淋

a stew[2]
[ə stju]
燉菜

1 **spaghetti** 這是義大利麵 pasta [`pɑstə] 中的一種，指的是中等粗細的長麵條。

2 **a stew** 燉菜是將肉和蔬菜放入鍋內後，在有湯的狀態下慢慢燉煮的料理，煮好的料理帶有濃郁的湯汁。

對話 抱怨就要理直氣壯

14-4

請聽以下對話，並跟著說說看。 14-4

送上來的義大利麵實在是鹹得不能再鹹，秀智打算抗議，便叫來了服務生。

秀智 Excuse me, but **this is too salty.**
[ɪk`skjuz mi bʌt ðɪs ɪz tu `sɔltɪ]

服務生 I'm sorry. Shall I bring you another one?
[aɪm `sɑrɪ ] [ ʃæl aɪ brɪŋ ju ə`nʌðɚ wʌn]

秀智 Yes, please. I can't eat this.
[jɛs pliz] [aɪ kænt it ðɪs]

過了一會兒，秀智吃完了新送來的食物，想要結帳，便叫來了服務生。

秀智 Check, please.
[tʃɛk pliz]

check 帳單

服務生 Here you go. The total is 35 dollars.
[hɪr ju go] [ðə `totəl ɪz `θɝtɪ faɪv `dɑləz]

秀智 Hmm, there is a problem with the bill.
[həm ðɛr ɪz ə `prɑbləm wɪð ðə bɪl]

I didn't order a salad.
[aɪ `dɪdənt `ɔrdɚ ə `sæləd]

服務生 I'm sorry. I'll be right back with the correct bill.
[aɪm `sɑrɪ ] [ aɪl bi raɪt bæk wɪð ðə kə`rɛkt bɪl]

秀智 不好意思，但**這個太鹹了。**
服務生 很抱歉。我再為你上一份好嗎？
秀智 好的，謝謝。這個我沒辦法吃。

秀智 （請給我）帳單，謝謝。
服務生 在這裡，總共是 35 美金。
秀智 嗯，帳單有問題呢。**我沒有點沙拉。**
服務生 對不起。我馬上拿正確的帳單過來。

驗收 14 對餐廳的不滿之處

解答在 219 頁

A 請從選項中選出能填入空格的單字。

選項 **order** | **salty** | **bring** | **salad**

① 這個太鹹了。

This is too ______.

② 我沒有點沙拉。

I didn't ______ a ______.

③ 我會把你點的餐點拿給你。

I'll ______ you what you ordered.

B 請在選項中找出適當的表達方式，並完成下列句子。

選項 **cold** | **tough** | **ice cream** | **spaghetti**

① 我沒有點義大利麵。

I didn't order ______.

② 我沒有點冰淇淋。

I didn't order ______.

③ 這個肉太韌了。

This is too ______.

④ 這個太涼了。

This is too ______.

15 速食餐廳

◎ 請聽以下對話，並跟著說說看。 15-1

對話A

店員 May I take your order?

[me aɪ tek jʊɚ `ɔrdɚ]

振洙 **I'd like** a cheeseburger.

[aɪd laɪk ə `tʃiz͵bɝgɚ]

對話B

店員 Do you want ice in your drink?

[du ju wɑnt aɪs ɪn jʊɚ drɪŋk]

秀智 **No** ice, **please**.

[no aɪs pliz]

句型 29 **I'd like +** 食物／飲料 **.** 我要～。

就像句型 16 所學過的一樣，「I'd like＋名詞」是客氣地表達「想要～」的句子。名詞部分如果帶入食物或飲料的名稱，就變成「我想要食物／飲料」，在餐廳裡就表示「請給我～」。也可以簡單地以 want [wɑnt] 表達這個意思，例如想點起司漢堡的時候，也可以說 I want a cheeseburger.。

句型 29 **我要一個起司漢堡。**

句型 30 **不要冰塊，謝謝。**

15-1

想簡單解決一餐時，沒有比速食餐廳更快速又方便的了。來熟悉在漢堡王、麥當勞等速食餐廳裡點餐時會用到的句型！

對話 A

店員　請問你要點餐了嗎？

振洙　我要一個起司漢堡。

對話 B

店員　你的飲料要加冰塊嗎？

秀智　不要冰塊，謝謝。

新出現的單字

take an order [tek æn `ɔrdɚ] 接受點餐

cheeseburger [`tʃiz͵bɝgɚ] 起司漢堡

want [wɑnt] 想要

ice [aɪs] 冰（塊）

drink [drɪŋk] 飲料

burger 是「漢堡」，cheeseburger 是指放了 cheese（起司）的漢堡。

句型 30 **No + 想去掉的東西 , please.** 不要／去掉～，謝謝。

點食物或飲料的時候，如果想要去掉某樣食材，只要活用 No（沒有～、不要～），和客氣地請求時使用的 please（請、拜託）就可以了。除了 No 之外，也可以用 Without [wɪ`ðaʊt]（沒有～、去掉～），如 Without ice, please. 這樣來表達。另外，使用動詞 hold [hold]（抓住、扣除）構成 Hold the ice, please.，也同樣是「請去掉冰塊」的意思。

句型29 練習

我要～。

15-2

○ 請將單字帶入空格內並說說看。 15-2

I'd like ☐.

我要 ☐ 。

a number 3[1]
[ə ˋnʌmbɚ θri]
一個 3 號餐

a chicken burger
[ə ˋtʃɪkɪn ˋbɝgɚ]
一個雞肉漢堡

a hot dog
[ə hɑt dɔg]
一個熱狗

a Whopper[2]
[ə ˋhwɑpɚ]
一個華堡

French fries
[frɛntʃ fraɪz]
炸薯條

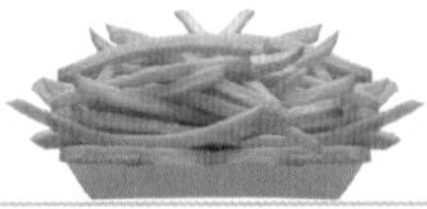

a biscuit
[ə ˋbɪskɪt]
一個比司吉（小麵包）

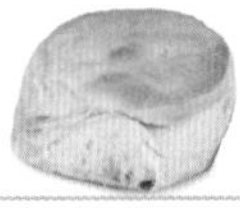

1 a number 3 包含飲料和炸薯條的套餐上若標有 number（號碼），點套餐時只要簡單地說號碼就可以了。此時，若只點一份套餐，前面請一定要加上 a 或 one。

2 a Whopper 是美國速食餐廳漢堡王（Burger King）最具代表性的漢堡，whopper 是「非常巨大」的意思。在麥當勞（McDonald's）則是賣 Big Mac [bɪg mæk]。

不要／去掉～，謝謝。

15-3

◎ 請將單字帶入空格內並說說看。 15-3

No ______, please.

不要／去掉 ______，謝謝。

ketchup [ˋkɛtʃəp] 番茄醬 	**mayo**[1] [ˋmeo] 美乃滋 	**syrup** [ˋsɪrəp] 糖漿 
whipped cream [hwɪpt krim] 鮮奶油	**onions** [ˋʌnjənz] 洋蔥 	**cucumber** [ˋkjukəmbɚ] 黃瓜 

■ **想去掉的醬料與材料**　除此之外可以要求去掉的材料還有 mustard [ˋmʌstɚd]「芥末」、pepper [ˋpɛpɚ]「胡椒」、cinnamon [ˋsɪnəmən]「肉桂」、carrot [ˋkærət]「胡蘿蔔」、parsley [ˋpɑrslɪ]「香芹」等。另外，也可以要求去掉東南亞料理中，香味強烈的 coriander [ˌkorɪˋændɚ]「香菜」及 cilantro [sɪˋlæntro]「香菜葉」。

1 **mayo**　是從 mayonnaise [ˌmeəˋnez]「美乃滋」縮寫而來的口語體單字。發音上請留意不是唸作 [mayo]。

對話 照自己的口味點餐

15-4

◎ 請聽以下對話，並跟著說說看。 15-4

振洙打算簡單地解決一餐，於是去了速食餐廳。

店員 Next, please.
[ˋnɛkst pliz]

next 下一個的

振洙 **I'd like a cheeseburger.**
[aɪd laɪk ə ˋtʃiz͵bɝgɚ]

店員 Anything to drink?
[ˋɛnɪ͵θɪŋ tu drɪŋk]

振洙 I'll have a medium Sprite. **No ice, please.**
[aɪl hæv ə ˋmidɪəm spraɪt] [no aɪs pliz]

店員 Do you want any side dishes?
[du ju wɑnt ˋɛnɪ saɪd dɪʃɪs]

振洙 No, thank you.
[no θæŋk ju]

店員 For here or to go?
[fɔr hɪr ɔr tu go]

振洙 For here, please.
[fɔr hɪr pliz]

店員 下一位。
振洙 **我要一個起司漢堡。**
店員 飲料呢？
振洙 我要一杯中杯的雪碧。**不要冰塊，謝謝。**
店員 你要副餐嗎？
振洙 不用，謝謝。
店員 內用還是外帶？
振洙 內用，謝謝。

驗收 15 速食餐廳

解答在 219 頁

A 請從選項中選出能填入空格的單字。

選項 **ice** | **take** | **like** | **order**

① 請問你要點餐了嗎？

May I ______ your ______?

② 我要一個起司漢堡。

I'd ______ a cheeseburger.

③ 不要冰塊，謝謝。

No ______, please.

B 請在選項中找出適當的表達方式，並完成下列句子。

選項 **a hot dog** | **onions** | **French fries** | **ketchup**

① 我要一根熱狗。

I'd like ______.

② 我要炸薯條。

I'd like ______.

③ 不要洋蔥，謝謝。

No ______, please.

④ 不要番茄醬，謝謝。

No ______, please.

16 咖啡廳

◎ 請聽以下對話，並跟著說說看。 16-1

對話A

店員 What can I get you?
[hwɑt kæn aɪ gɛt ju]

秀智 **I'll have** a latte.
[aɪl hæv ə `lɑte]

對話B

振洙 **Can you give me** a sleeve?
[kæn ju gɪv mi ə sliv]

店員 Sure. Here you are.
[ʃʊr] [hɪr ju ɑr]

句型 31 **I'll have +** 食物／飲料 **.** 我要～。

I'll 是 I will（我將要～）的縮寫，用來表示自己將要做某件事的意志。動詞 have 不只表示「擁有」，也是「吃、喝」的意思，在餐廳或咖啡廳裡點餐的時候說 I'll have ~. 的話，就變成「我要吃～、我要喝～」的意思，因此在點餐時，就能用來傳達「我要～」的意圖。

句型 31 我要一杯拿鐵。

句型 32 你可以給我一個杯套嗎？

16-1

雖然在咖啡廳點咖啡好像很難，但其實比想像中簡單。來認識點咖啡時可以使用的句型，並認識各式各樣的咖啡吧！

對話 A

店員　你要來點什麼？

秀智　我要一杯拿鐵。

對話 B

振洙　你可以給我一個杯套嗎？

店員　當然，在這裡。

新出現的單字

latte [\`lɑte]
拿鐵（加了牛奶的咖啡）

sleeve [sliv]
杯套（套在杯子上的厚紙板）

latte 是義大利文 caffé latte（咖啡拿鐵）的縮寫。caffé 是「咖啡」，latte 則是「牛奶」。在歐洲只說 latte 的話，有可能只會給你牛奶，因此請仔細看過菜單再點餐。

句型 32 Can you give me + 物品 ? 你可以給我～嗎？

這是活用向他人拜託某事的句型「Can you＋動詞?」和動詞 give（給）的句型，是拜託對方給自己某樣物品時使用的句型。give 有兩種句型可以使用：「give＋人＋物品」或「give＋物品＋to＋人」，在這裡因為表示人的 me（我，I 的受格）接在 give 之後，所以物品必須直接接在人的後面。

句型31 練習

我要～。

16-2

◎ 請將單字帶入空格內並說說看。 16-2

I'll have ______.

我要______。

an espresso
[æn ɛs`prɛso]
一杯義式濃縮咖啡

an Americano
[æn əmɛrɪ`kɑno]
一杯美式咖啡

a cappuccino
[ə ˏkɑpə`tʃino]
一杯卡布奇諾

a cafe mocha
[ə kə`fe `mokə]
一杯摩卡咖啡

an iced tea
[æn aɪst ti]
一杯冰茶

a hot chocolate
[ə hɑt `tʃɑkəlɪt]
一杯熱巧克力、可可亞

■ **各式各樣的咖啡** 義式濃縮咖啡是利用滾燙的蒸氣，瞬間加熱磨細的咖啡粉所萃取出來的咖啡。美式咖啡則是義式濃縮咖啡加熱水製成的咖啡，因為是二戰時美國人（American）在義大利喝的咖啡，所以得到這樣的名稱。卡布奇諾是義式濃縮咖啡加入一些牛奶，再填滿奶泡的咖啡，上面會撒上可可粉或肉桂粉來飲用。另外，摩卡咖啡則是義式濃縮咖啡和牛奶、巧克力糖漿或巧克力粉混合製成的咖啡。

句型32 練習

你可以給我～嗎？

16-3

請將單字帶入空格內並說說看。 16-3

Can you give me ______ ?

你可以給我 ______ 嗎？

a straw
[ə strɔ]
一根吸管

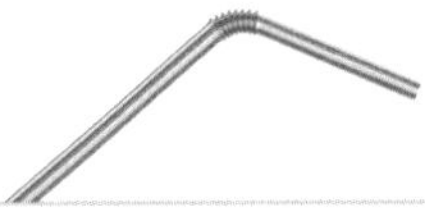

a fork[1]
[ə fɔrk]
一支叉子

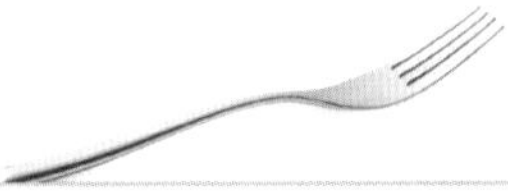

a lid
[ə lɪd]
一個杯蓋

a receipt
[ə rɪ`sit]
收據

some napkins
[sʌm `næpkɪnz]
一些餐巾紙

some sugar[2]
[sʌm `ʃʊgɚ]
一些糖

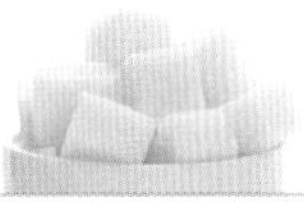

1 a fork 除了叉子外，在餐廳或咖啡廳可以索取的餐具還有 spoon [spun]（叉子）、knife [naɪf]（刀子）、chopsticks [`tʃɑp͵stɪks]（筷子）等。

2 some sugar some 出現在名詞的前面時，表示「一些、一點」。除了 sugar 之外，也請帶入 salt [sɔlt]（鹽）、pepper [`pɛpɚ]（胡椒）等各種調味料說說看。

對話 一杯咖啡的悠閒

16-4

◎ 請聽以下對話，並跟著說說看。 16-4

吃飽飯之後，就很想喝咖啡。秀智為了喝咖啡進入了咖啡廳。

秀智 **I'll have a latte.**
[aɪl hæv ə `lɑte]

店員 What size?
[hwɑt saɪz]

秀智 Large, please.
[lɑrdʒ pliz]

large 大的

店員 Hot or iced?
[hɑt ɔr aɪst]

iced 放了冰塊的

秀智 Hot, please.
[hɑt pliz]

店員 For here or to go?
[fɔr hɪr ɔr tu go]

秀智 To go, please.
[tu go pliz]

店員 Okay. Here is your coffee.
[ˌo`ke ] [ hɪr ɪz jʊɚ `kɔfɪ]

秀智 **Can you give me a sleeve?** It's too hot.
[kæn ju gɪv mi ə sliv] [ɪts tu hɑt]

秀智 **我要一杯拿鐵。**
店員 要哪個大小？
秀智 （請給我）大杯的，謝謝。
店員 要熱的還是要冰的？
秀智 （請給我）熱的，謝謝。
店員 這裡用還是帶走？
秀智 帶走，謝謝。
店員 好的，你的咖啡在這裡。
秀智 **你可以給我一個杯套嗎？**太燙了。

驗收 16 咖啡廳

解答在 220 頁

A 請從選項中選出能填入空格的單字。

選項 **sleeve** | **have** | **get** | **give**

① 你要來點什麼？

What can I ______ you?

② 我要一杯拿鐵。

I'll ______ a latte.

③ 你可以給我一個杯套嗎？

Can you ______ me a ______?

B 請在選項中找出適當的表達方式，並完成下列句子。

選項 **a straw** | **some sugar** | **a cappuccino** | **an espresso**

① 我要一杯義式濃縮咖啡。

I'll have ______.

② 我要一杯卡布奇諾。

I'll have ______.

③ 你可以給我一根吸管嗎？

Can you give me ______?

④ 你可以給我一些糖嗎？

Can you give me ______?

16-5

reserved 已預訂的

動詞 reserve [rɪ`zɝv] 表示「預訂」，過去分詞 reserved [rɪ`zɝvd] 則是表示「被預訂的」。餐廳會在已經被預訂的桌上放上有這個字的牌子。

Please wait to be seated 請等候帶位

wait 是「等待」、「be seated」是「就座的」的意思，所以 Please wait to be seated [pliz wet tu bi `sitɪd] 意思就是在引導入座前請稍等，是在餐廳入口常見到的標誌。

Order here 請在這裡點餐

order 是「點餐」，here 則是「這裡」，因此 Order here [`ɔrdɚ hɪr] 是「請在這裡點餐」的意思。是在咖啡廳或速食店的點餐處常可以見到的語句。

Today's special 今日特餐

today's [tə`dez] 是「今天的」，special [`spɛʃəl] 當名詞是「特別的東西」，所以 Today's special [tə`dez `spɛʃəl] 就是表示「今日特餐」。另外 Chef's suggestions [ʃɛfs sə`dʒɛstʃənz] 是「主廚推薦」，即餐廳所推薦的料理。

drive-through [thru] 得來速

drive 是「駕駛」，through 是「通過～」的意思，在駕著車的狀態下點餐並外帶的服務就稱為 drive-through [ˋdraɪvˏθru]，一般會將 through 縮寫標示成 thru。主要可以在像星巴克這樣的連鎖咖啡廳或速食店使用這項服務。

pub 酒吧

為 public house（直譯：大眾之家）的縮寫，指的是從酒類、各種飲料到食物皆販售的大眾酒館，是在英國很常見的酒吧形式，多半是人們社交、放鬆的場合，和專門賣酒不賣餐食的 bar 略有不同。

BYO 自己帶酒

BYO 是在酒類販售規定嚴格的澳洲常見的餐廳形式，表示因為沒有販酒執照，所以客人可以直接帶酒進去的餐廳。BYO 是 Bring your own [brɪŋ jʊɚ on] 的縮寫，bring 是「帶來」，your own 是「你自己的」。

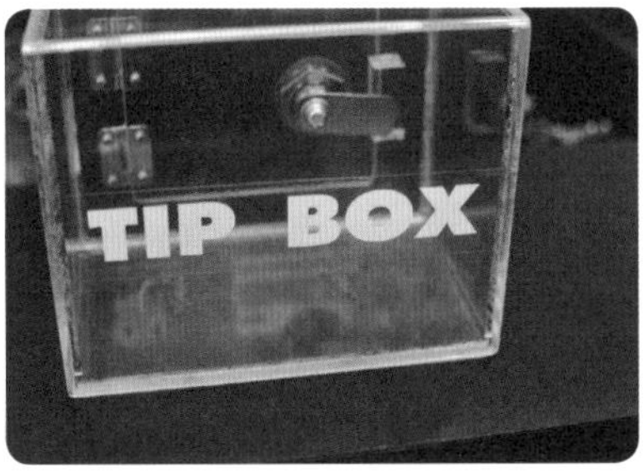

tip box 小費箱

在美國和加拿大，額外給餐廳服務生帳單上所寫金額約 15~20% 的 tip（小費）是一種習慣。雖然在速食餐廳或咖啡廳不需要額外給小費，但店家可能也會在櫃台準備放小費的 box（箱子）。

生動的旅遊情報

仔細看看英文菜單

點餐時看菜單，
因為有許多不熟悉的單字，
所以很多時候點餐會碰上困難。
請熟悉下列單字後，
有自信地點餐吧！

菜單

appetizer [`æpə͵taɪzɚ] 開胃菜
（在用餐前為了提振食慾而喝的酒或所吃的簡單料理）

entrée [`ɑntre] 主菜
（多指餐廳或晚餐的主菜，在很正式的餐廳則是指上主菜前的小菜）

main dish [men dɪʃ] 主菜

side dish [saɪd dɪʃ] 配菜

dessert [dɪ`zɝt] 甜點、餐後點心

seafood [`si͵fud] 海鮮料理

meat [mit] 肉類

soup [sup] 湯

salad [`sæləd] 沙拉

sandwich [`sændwɪtʃ] 三明治

burger [`bɝgɚ] 漢堡

pizza [`pitsə] 披薩

pasta [`pɑstə] 義大利麵

noodle [`nudəl] 麵

drink / beverage
[drɪŋk / `bɛvərɪdʒ] 飲料

vegetarian menu
[͵vɛdʒə`tɛrɪən `mɛnju] 素食餐點

肉類

beef [bif] 牛肉

pork [pɔrk] 豬肉

poultry [`poltrɪ] 家禽類
（雞肉、鴨肉、火雞肉等）

chicken [`tʃɪkɪn] 雞肉

duck [dʌk] 鴨肉

turkey [`tɝkɪ] 火雞肉

mutton [`mʌtən] 羊肉

lamb [læm] 羔羊肉

steak [stek] 牛排

海鮮類

salmon [`sæmən] 鮭魚

cod [kɑd] 鱈魚

catfish [`kæt͵fɪʃ] 鯰魚

sea bass [si bæs] 鱸魚

oyster [`ɔɪstɚ] 牡蠣

clam [klæm] 蛤蜊

mussel [`mʌsəl] 淡菜

lobster [`lɑbstɚ] 龍蝦

shrimp / prawn [ʃrɪmp / prɔn] 蝦

crab [kræb] 螃蟹

蔬菜

mushroom [`mʌʃrʊm] 蘑菇

carrot [`kærət] 胡蘿蔔

potato [pə`teto] 馬鈴薯

sweet potato [swit pə`teto] 地瓜

onion [`ʌnjən] 洋蔥

cabbage [`kæbɪdʒ] 高麗菜

spinach [`spɪnɪtʃ] 波菜

broccoli [`brɑkəlɪ] 花椰菜

pumpkin [`pʌmpkɪn] 南瓜

飲料

hot drink [hɑt drɪŋk] 熱飲

cold drink [kold drɪŋk] 冷飲

alcoholic [ˌælkə`hɔlɪk] 含酒精的

non-alcoholic [nɑn ˌælkə`hɔlɪk]
無酒精的

red wine [rɛd waɪn]
紅酒（紅葡萄酒）

white wine [hwaɪt waɪn]
白酒（白葡萄酒）

bottled beer [`bɑtəld bɪr] 瓶裝啤酒

draft / draught beer [dræft bɪr]
生啤酒（美式／英式拼寫，兩字發音相同）

cocktail [`kɑkˌtel] 雞尾酒
（由多種飲料混合而成的酒或飲料）

soft drink [sɔft drɪŋk] 軟性飲料
（不含酒精的飲料）

Coke [kok] 可樂

Sprite [spraɪt] 雪碧

Fanta [`fæntə] 芬達

juice [dʒus] 果汁

甜點

ice cream [aɪs krim] 冰淇淋

apple pie [`æpəl paɪ] 蘋果派

cheesecake [`tʃizˌkek] 起司蛋糕

chocolate cake [`tʃɑkəlɪt kek]
巧克力蛋糕

pudding [`pʊdɪŋ] 布丁
（牛奶、雞蛋和砂糖等做成的甜點）

tart [tɑrt] 塔
（上面放了水果或甜品的派）

其他

toast [tost] 吐司

pancake [`pænˌkek] 鬆餅

bread [brɛd] 麵包

ham [hæm] 火腿

bacon [`bekən] 培根

egg [ɛg] 雞蛋

omelet [`ɑmlɪt] 歐姆蛋
（混入蔬菜或火腿、培根等的雞蛋料理）

curry [`kɝɪ] 咖哩

cheese [tʃiz] 起司

生動的旅遊情報

牛排的熟度

在外國點牛排的話，
服務生一定會
詢問牛排的熟度。
請好好熟悉與牛排熟度
相關的單字，
並在點餐時試著運用吧！

blue rare [blu rɛr] 近生

最生的狀態，指僅僅在高溫下稍微煎一煎表面，中間幾乎是接近生肉的感覺，一般的餐廳不常販售。

rare [rɛr] 一分熟

只有表面是熟的，牛排中間有 75% 是紅色的狀態。充滿肉汁，可以享受到柔軟的肉質。

medium rare [`midɪəm rɛr] 三分熟

外皮是熟透的灰褐色，牛排中間有 50% 是紅色的狀態。表面因為經過一定程度煎烤，口感焦脆，裡頭保留了肉汁，可以品嘗肉的風味。

medium [`midɪəm] 五分熟

表面雖然完全熟透，但是中間有 25% 是粉紅色的狀態。雖然肉汁較少，但可以感受到嚼勁。

medium well [`midɪəm wɛl] 七分熟

也稱作 medium well-done [`midɪəm wɛl dʌn]。比五分熟更熟，中間透著介於粉紅色和灰色中間的顏色。

well-done [wɛl dʌn] 全熟

連內部都完全熟透，幾乎沒有肉汁的狀態。雖然肉質可能會變得又硬又韌，但是不敢吃不夠熟或帶血水的肉的人，還是選這個比較好。

購物時

17 買衣服

18 殺價

19 換貨與退貨

17 買衣服

◎ 請聽以下對話，並跟著說說看。 17-1

對話A

店員 Can I help you?
[kæn aɪ hɛlp ju]

振洙 **I'm looking for** a jacket.
[aɪm ˋlʊkɪŋ fɔr ə ˋdʒækɪt]

對話B

振洙 **Do you have this in** a bigger size?
[du ju hæv ðɪs ɪn ə ˋbɪgɚ saɪz]

店員 Here is a Large.
[hɪr ɪz ə lɑrdʒ]

句型 33 **I'm looking for + 物品 .** 我正在找～。

look for 是「尋找～」，I'm looking for ~. 可以表示自己正在找某樣東西。進到商店裡，店員如果詢問 May [Can] I help you?（需要幫忙嗎？）或是 Do you need anything?（你需要什麼嗎？），請利用這個句型來說明自己想找的東西。

句型 33 我正在找一件夾克。

句型 34 （你們）這個有更大的尺寸嗎？

17-1

◎ 購物是旅行中的一大樂趣，有時也能用比在台灣更便宜的價格購入商品。快來熟悉買衣服時常用的句型吧！

對話 A

店員　需要幫忙嗎？

振洙　我正在找一件夾克（我想買夾克）。

對話 B

振洙　（你們）這個有更大的尺寸嗎？

店員　這裡有一件 L 號的。

新出現的單字

look for [lʊk fɔr] 尋找～

jacket [ˋdʒækɪt] 夾克

bigger [ˋbɪgɚ] 更大的

size [saɪz] 大小、尺寸

large [lɑrdʒ] 大的

big 是意為「大的」的形容詞，加上 er 的 bigger 時，就變成比較級，有「更大的」的意思。

句型 34 Do you have this in + 尺寸／顏色 ?

（你們）這個有～的嗎？

Do you have this? 直譯的話是「你們有這個嗎？」，後面加上「in＋尺寸／顏色」，表示「這個有～尺寸／顏色的嗎？」，也就是具體詢問特定產品的尺寸或顏色的句子。也可以像 Do you have this in blue in a Large?（這個有 L 號藍色的嗎？）一樣，同時詢問尺寸和顏色。

句型33 練習

我正在找～。

17-2

◎ 請將單字帶入空格內並說說看。 17-2

I'm looking for ______.

我正在找 ______ 。

a shirt
[ə ʃɝt]
一件襯衫

a blouse
[ə blaʊz]
一件女用襯衫

a vest
[ə vɛst]
一件背心

a coat
[ə kot]
一件大衣

jeans[1]
[dʒinz]
牛仔褲

shorts[1]
[ʃɔrts]
短褲

■ **多樣的衣物種類** 除了上面出現的單字之外，還有 underwear [`ʌndɚ͵wɛr]（內衣褲）、sweater [`swɛtɚ]（毛衣）、dress [drɛs]（洋裝）、skirt [skɝt]（裙子），也請一起記下來。

1 **jeans / shorts** 褲子因為有右左兩隻褲管，所以即使只有一件，也視為複數，單字後面要加上 s 或 es 變成複數型。腳伸進去的部分有兩個的 underpants [`ʌndɚ͵pænts]（內褲）、stockings [`stɑkɪŋz]（長襪）也是一樣。

句型34 練習

（你們）這個有～的嗎？

17-3

請將單字帶入空格內並說說看。 17-3

Do you have this in ______?

（你們）這個有 ______ 的嗎？

a Medium[1]
[ə `midɪəm]
M 號

a size 8[2]
[ə saɪz et]
8 號

a smaller size
[ə smɔlɚ saɪz]
更小號的

red
[rɛd]
紅色

black
[blæk]
黑色

beige
[beʒ]
米色

1 a Medium 通常衣服尺寸分為 S（小）、M（中）、L（大），分別是取 small [smɔl]（小的）、medium [`midɪəm]（中間的）和 large [lɑrdʒ]（大的）的開頭字母而來。另外，比 L 更大的 XL 是從 extra large [`ɛkstrə lɑrdʒ]，比 S 更小的 XS 是從 extra small [`ɛkstrə smɔl] 而來的。

2 a size 8 這是在美國會使用的尺碼規格，從 0 開始，每個尺碼的數字差 2，如 size 8、size 6。size 8、6 大約與 L、M 號尺寸差不多。

對話 買最適合我的衣服

17-4

◎ 請聽以下對話，並跟著說說看。 17-4

秀智出國玩只帶了輕薄的衣物，但當地的風勢卻比預期的更猛烈。她為了買外套去了趟服飾店。

店員 May I help you?
[me aɪ hɛlp ju]

秀智 **I'm looking for a jacket.**
[aɪm `lʊkɪŋ fɔr ə `dʒækɪt]

店員 How about this one?
[haʊ ə`baʊt ðɪs wʌn]

秀智 I like it. Can I try it on?
[aɪ laɪk ɪt] [kæn aɪ traɪ ɪt ɑn]

try on 試穿

店員 Sure.
[ʃʊr]

秀智 Well, it's too tight.
[wɛl ɪts tu taɪt]

Do you have this in a bigger size?
[du ju hæv ðɪs ɪn ə `bɪgɚ saɪz]

tight 緊的

店員 Let me see.... Here you are.
[lɛt mi si] [hɪr ju ɑr]

秀智 Oh, it's perfect. I'll take it.
[o ɪts `pɝfɪkt] [aɪl tek ɪt]

perfect 完美的

店員 需要幫忙嗎？
秀智 **我正在找一件夾克（我想買夾克）。**
店員 這件如何？
秀智 我很喜歡。我可以試穿嗎？
店員 當然。
秀智 嗯，它太緊了。**（你們）這個有更大的尺寸嗎？**
店員 我看一下……在這裡。
秀智 噢，太完美了（剛剛好）。我要這件。

驗收 17 買衣服

解答在 220 頁

A 請從選項中選出能填入空格的單字。

選項 **bigger** | **Large** | **looking** | **jacket**

① 我正在找一件夾克。

I'm ______ for a ______.

② （你們）這個有更大的尺寸嗎？

Do you have this in a ______ size?

③ 這裡有一件 L 號的。

Here is a ______.

B 請在選項中找出適當的表達方式，並完成下列句子。

選項 **jeans** | **a Medium** | **a vest** | **black**

① 我正在找一件背心。

I'm looking for ______.

② 我正在找牛仔褲。

I'm looking for ______.

③ （你們）這個有黑色的嗎？

Do you have this in ______?

④ （你們）這個有 M 號的嗎？

Do you have this in ______?

18 殺價

◎ 請聽以下對話，並跟著說說看。 18-1

對話A

秀智 **How much is** this watch?
[haʊ mʌtʃ ɪz ðɪs wɑtʃ]

店員 It's 20 dollars.
[ɪts `twɛntɪ `dɑlɚz]

對話B

振洙 **Are these** watches **on sale**?
[ɑr ðiz wɑtʃɪz ɑn sel]

店員 Yes, all items are 10 percent off.
[jɛs ɔl `aɪtəmz ɑr tɛn pɚ`sɛnt ɔf]

句型 35 How much is [are] + 物品 ? ～多少錢？

How much 表示「（價格）多少」，是在問價錢的時候使用的句型。物品是一個（單數）時，要以 How much is ~? 提問；若物品有很多個（複數）時，則用 How much are ~? 提問。請注意，有些物品就算只有一個，仍視為複數，如 jeans（牛仔褲）、sunglasses [`sʌn͵glæsɪz]（太陽眼鏡），這時要以 How much are ~? 提問。而物品的數量也會影響這個句型的回答：當物品是一個時，以 It is ~. 回答；而物品為多個時，則以 They are ~. 來回答。

句型 35 這隻手錶多少錢？

句型 36 這些手錶在特價嗎？

18-1

買東西的時候，最令人考慮的因素應該就是價格了。來認識在店裡詢問物品價錢，及確認是否正在特價的表達方式吧！

對話 A

秀智　這隻手錶多少錢？

店員　20 美元。

對話 B

振洙　這些手錶在特價嗎？

店員　是的，所有商品都打 9 折。

新出現的單字

how much [haʊ mʌtʃ]（價格）多少

watch [wɑtʃ] 手錶

on sale [ɑn sel] 特價中的

item [`aɪtəm] 商品、品項

percent [pɚ`sɛnt] 百分比

off [ɔf] 折扣

句型 36 Are these + 物品 + on sale? 這些～在特價嗎？

on sale 表示「特價」，是用來詢問商品是否特價的字詞。如果要問一樣物品是否特價時，可以用 Is this ~? 來問，如 Is this hat on sale?（這頂帽子在特價嗎？）；如果是問多個物品是否特價時，則要以 Are these ~? 來詢問，如 Are these hats on sale?（這些帽子在特價嗎？）。請注意單複數的一致，如 these 後要接 hats（帽子們）這樣的名詞複數型。

句型35 練習

～多少錢？

18-2

◎ 請將單字帶入空格內並說說看。 18-2

How much is [are] ______?

______ 多少錢？

this tie
[ðɪs taɪ]
這條領帶

this lipstick
[ðɪs `lɪp͵stɪk]
這支唇膏

this perfume
[ðɪs pɚ`fjum]
這瓶香水

these shoes[1]
[ðiz ʃuz]
這雙鞋

these gloves[1]
[ðiz glʌvz]
這雙手套

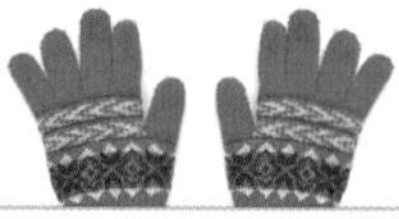

these sunglasses[1]
[ðiz `sʌn͵glæsɪz]
這副太陽眼鏡

■ **this / these** this 和 these 兩者都是在指示較靠近自己的東西時使用的字，表示「這～」。當東西只有一個的時候用 this，多個的時候用 these。

1 **shoes / gloves / sunglasses** 由兩個組合成一雙的物品，在單字後面要加上 s 或 es。鞋子、手套、眼鏡都是左邊、右邊各一個，所以視為一雙，當字尾是 s、z、x、ch、sh 時，加 es，其他狀況多半直接加 s。

句型36 練習

這些～在特價嗎？

18-3

◎ 請將單字帶入空格內並說說看。 18-3

Are these ______ on sale?

這些 ______ 在特價嗎？

T-shirts
[ti ʃɝts]
T 恤

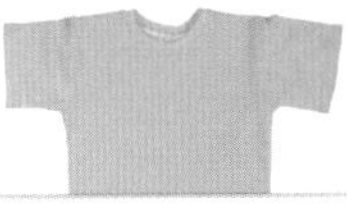

suits
[suts]
西裝

earrings[1]
[ˋɪr͵rɪŋz]
耳環

caps
[kæps]
鴨舌帽

belts
[bɛlts]
皮帶

socks
[sɑks]
襪子

■ **多樣的飾品** 飾品的英文是 accessory [ækˋsɛsərɪ]，請一併記下 ring [rɪŋ]（戒指）、bracelet [ˋbreslɪt]（手環）、necklace [ˋnɛklɪs]（項鍊）、hairpin [ˋhɛr͵pɪn]（髮夾）、hairband [ˋhɛrbænd]（髮圈）等各種飾品的名稱。

1 earrings ear 是「耳朵」，ring 是「戒指、環」，因此 earrings 是指戴在耳朵上的環，即「耳環」。因為是戴在兩隻耳朵上，要使用複數型。

對話 購物時殺價是基本功

18-4

◎ 請聽以下對話，並跟著說說看。 18-4

振洙在購物商場裡逛街的時候，發現了中意的手錶。

振洙 Excuse me. **Are these watches on sale?**
[ɪk`skjuz mi] [ɑr ðiz watʃɪz ɑn sel]

店員 No, we just started selling them.
[no wi dʒʌst `stɑrtɪd `sɛlɪŋ ðɛm]

start 開始

振洙 Then, **how much is this watch?**
[ðɛn haʊ mʌtʃ ɪz ðɪs watʃ]

店員 It's 200 dollars.
[ɪts tu `hʌndrəd `dɑlɚz]

hundred 百

振洙 Oh, that's too expensive.
[o ðæts tu ɪk`spɛnsɪv]

expensive 貴的

Can you come down a little bit?
[kæn ju kʌm daʊn ə `lɪtəl bɪt]

come down 降低（價格）

店員 Okay. I will give you a 5-percent discount.
[ˏo`ke ] [ aɪ wɪl gɪv ju ə faɪv pɚ`sɛnt `dɪskaʊnt]

振洙 Sounds good. I'll take it.
[saʊndz gʊd] [aɪl tek ɪt]

振洙 不好意思，**這些手錶在特價嗎？**
店員 沒有，我們才剛開始販售它們。
振洙 那麼，**這支手錶多少錢呢？**
店員 200 美金。
振洙 噢，這太貴了。你可以稍微降價一點（給點折扣）嗎？
店員 好的。我給你打 95 折吧。
振洙 聽起來很棒。我要買這個。

驗收 18 殺價

解答在 220 頁

A 請從選項中選出能填入空格的單字。

選項 **dollars** | **sale** | **much** | **watch**

① 這隻手錶多少錢？

How ______ is this ______?

② 20 美金。

It's 20 ______.

③ 這些手錶在特價嗎？

Are these watches on ______?

B 請在選項中找出適當的表達方式，並完成下列句子。

選項 **these shoes** | **socks** | **this tie** | **earrings**

① 這條領帶多少錢？

How much is ______?

② 這雙鞋子多少錢？

How much are ______?

③ 這些襪子在特價嗎？

Are these ______ on sale?

④ 這些耳環在特價嗎？

Are these ______ on sale?

19 換貨與退貨

◎ 請聽以下對話，並跟著說說看。 19-1

對話A

振洙 **Can I exchange this for** a bigger size?

[kæn aɪ ɪks`tʃendʒ ðɪs fɔr ə `bɪgɚ saɪz]

店員 Let me check for you.

[lɛt mi tʃɛk fɔr ju]

對話B

秀智 **I'd like to get a refund on** this skirt.

[aɪd laɪk tu gɛt ə `riˏfʌnd ɑn ðɪs skɝt]

店員 Sorry, but you can only exchange it.

[`sɑrɪ bʌt ju kæn `onlɪ ɪks`tʃendʒ ɪt]

句型 37 **Can I exchange this for + 想要的東西 ?**

我可以把這個可以換成～嗎？

「Can I＋動詞?」是「可以～嗎？」的意思，用來詢問一件事情的可能性。exchange 是意為「交換、更換」的動詞。如果問 Can I exchange this?，就是「我可以換這個嗎？」的意思。這時若在後面以介系詞 for 帶出想要的顏色或尺寸，就能具體詢問可否更換成該商品。

句型 37 我可以把這個換成更大的尺寸嗎？
句型 38 我想退這件裙子。

19-1

購物後，如果東西有問題，請不要慌張，去退換貨就好。來學習在商店裡退換貨時可以使用的句型吧！

對話 A

振洙　我可以把這個換成更大的尺寸嗎？

職員　我幫你確認一下。

對話 B

秀智　我想退這件裙子（我想得到這件裙子的退款）。

職員　不好意思，但你只能換貨。

新出現的單字

exchange [ɪks`tʃendʒ] 交換

check [tʃɛk] 確認

refund [`riˌfʌnd] 退款、退費

skirt [skɝt] 裙子

only [`onlɪ] 僅有、只有

get 是「接受、獲得」的意思，get a refund 就成了「得到退款」。

句型 38 I'd like to get a refund on + 物品 . 我想退～。

get a refund 是「得到退款」，後面如果放入「on＋物品」的話，就能表達要求退回某物品的意思。在這裡雖然是用「I'd like to＋動詞.（我想要～）」句型，但是也能利用前面學過的「Can I＋動詞?」，以「Can I get a refund on＋物品?（我可以退～嗎？）」來提問。

句型37 練習

我可以把這個換成～嗎？

19-2

請將單字帶入空格內並說說看。 19-2

Can I exchange this for ______?

我可以把這個換成______嗎？

a different size
[ə ˋdɪfərənt saɪz]
其他尺寸

a different color
[ə ˋdɪfərənt ˋkʌlɚ]
其他顏色

a blue one[1]
[ə blu wʌn]
藍色的

a white one
[ə hwaɪt wʌn]
白色的

1 a blue one 這裡的 one 不是「一個」，而是代名詞，表示「（一個）東西（thing）」，因此 a blue one 是「藍色的東西」的意思。除了 blue（藍色的）之外，也可以帶入如 red [rɛd]（紅色的）、orange [ˋɔrɪndʒ]（橘色的）、purple [ˋpɝpəl]（紫色的）、pink [pɪŋk]（粉紅色的）、indigo [ˋɪn͵dɪgo]（靛藍色的）、yellow [ˋjɛlo]（黃色的）、beige [beʒ]（米色的）等各種顏色，來完成句子。

句型38 練習

我想退～。

19-3

請將單字帶入空格內並說說看。 19-3

I'd like to get a refund on ______.

我想退______。

this scarf
[ðɪs skɑrf]
這條圍巾

this dress
[ðɪs drɛs]
這件洋裝

this hat
[ðɪs hæt]
這頂帽子

these pajamas[1]
[ðiz pə`dʒæməz]
這套睡衣

these pants
[ðiz pænts]
這條褲子

these sandals[2]
[ðiz `sændəlz]
這雙涼鞋

1 **these pajamas** pajamas 是指睡覺時穿的上衣和褲子所組成的一套睡衣，因此視為複數，後面要加上 s。

2 **these sandals** 如同前面說明過的，成雙的褲子和鞋子類後面要加上 s 或 es。this sandal 是代表「這隻涼鞋」，these sandals 才是「這雙涼鞋」的意思。

對話 不能換貨的話就退款

19-4

請聽以下對話，並跟著說說看。 19-4

昨天因為便宜而衝動購買的裙子不合身，秀智又重新回到商店裡。

秀智 Excuse me. I’d like to exchange this skirt.
[ɪk`skjuz mi ] [ aɪd laɪk tu ɪks`tʃendʒ ðɪs skɝt]

店員 Is there something the matter with it?
[ɪz ðɛr `sʌmθɪŋ ðə `mætɚ wɪð ɪt]

秀智 It doesn’t fit me.
[ɪt `dʌzənt fɪt mi]

fit（大小）合適

Can I exchange this for a bigger size?
[kæn aɪ ɪks`tʃendʒ ðɪs for ə `bɪgɚ saɪz]

店員 I’m sorry, but we’re sold out.
[aɪm `sɑrɪ bʌt wɪr sold aʊt]

sold out（物品）賣光的

秀智 Then, **I’d like to get a refund on this skirt.**
[ðɛn aɪd laɪk tu gɛt ə `ri͵fʌnd ɑn ðɪs skɝt]

店員 Okay. Do you have your receipt?
[͵o`ke ] [ du ju hæv jʊɚ rɪ`sit]

秀智 Here you are.
[hɪr ju ɑr]

秀智 不好意思，我想換這件裙子。
店員 這件裙子有什麼問題嗎？
秀智 對我來說不合身。**我可以把這個換成更大的尺寸嗎？**
店員 很抱歉，我們這件賣完了。
秀智 那麼，**我想要退這件裙子。**
店員 好的。你有帶收據來嗎？
秀智 在這裡。

驗收 19 換貨與退貨

解答在 221 頁

A 請從選項中選出能填入空格的單字。

選項　**refund** | **bigger** | **exchange** | **skirt**

① 我可以把這個換成更大的尺寸嗎？
Can I exchange this for a ______ size?

② 我想退這件裙子。
I'd like to get a ______ on this ______.

③ 不好意思，但你只能換貨。
I'm sorry, but you can only ______ it.

B 請在選項中找出適當的表達方式，並完成下列句子。

選項　**these pants** | **a different size** | **a blue one** | **this hat**

① 我可以把這個換成其他尺寸嗎？
Can I exchange this for ______?

② 我可以把這個換成藍色的嗎？
Can I exchange this for ______?

③ 我想退這頂帽子。
I'd like to get a refund on ______.

④ 我想退這條褲子。
I'd like to get a refund on ______.

19-5

Open / Closed 營業中／休息中

這是經常能在商店門口看到的標誌，open [`opən] 是「開啟的」的意思，代表營業中。相反的 closed [klozd] 則是「關著的」的意思，表示打烊了。

Clearance sale 清倉特賣

clearance [`klɪrəns] 是「清除、整理」，在後面加上 sale [sel] 的話，就是指「清倉特賣」。由於是要清理庫存，所以物品會以低價賣出。

Buy 2 get 1 free 買二送一

buy 是「買」，get 是「得到」，free 則是「免費」的意思，Buy 2 get 1 free [baɪ tu gɛt wʌn fri] 是指如果買兩個則免費得到一個。另外，buy 1 get 1 free（買一送一）也是很常能看見的折扣文案。

50% off 打對折

off 是「掉下、降下」，「～% off」則表示價格調降百分之～的意思。up to ~% off 也很常見，是指「優惠高達百分之～」。

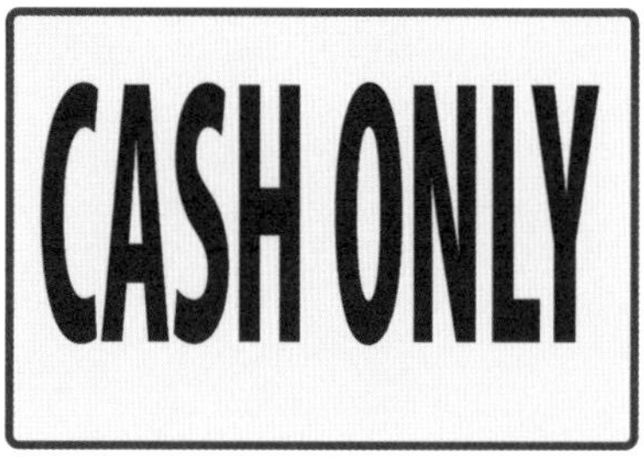

Cash only 僅收現金

cash 是「現金」，only 則是「只有、僅有」，而 cash only [kæʃ `onlɪ] 就是指在結帳時，只能使用現金支付的意思。

No refunds 不可退費

refund 是「退費」的意思，前面加上 No 的話就變成了「不可退費」。另外「不可換貨」是 No exchanges。這是通常在特賣商品上可以看到的文句。

Cashier 收銀員

cashier [kæ`ʃɪr] 是商店中處理金錢（cash）並負責結帳的「收銀員」的意思。在購物中心或賣場要表示結帳台的時候，也會使用這個單字。

Fitting room 試衣間

fitting 是「（衣服）合身的；試穿」的意思，而 room 則是「房間」。因此 fitting room [`fɪtɪŋ rum] 是指試穿衣服是否合適的「試衣間」，也稱為 dressing room [`drɛsɪŋ rum]。

生動的旅遊情報

美國的貨幣單位

台灣的新台幣
以「元」作為貨幣單位，
美國美金的貨幣單位
除了「元」之外
則還有「分」。
來認識美國的貨幣單位吧！

dollar [ˋdɑlɚ] 元

不只在美國，「元」也是在加拿大、澳洲、紐西蘭、新加坡、香港等各個國家使用的貨幣單位。要區分是哪個國家的貨幣時，會在前面冠上國家的名稱，如美元是 U.S. dollar、加拿大元是 Canadian dollar、澳元是 Australian dollar。代表符號是 $，在美國有 $1、$2、$5、$10、$20、$50 和 $100 元的紙幣，「元」裡面最小的 1 美元是以銅版發行。另外，2 美元是不容易見到的紙幣，也因此視為是幸運的象徵。

cent [sɛnt] 分

在美國也有比元更小一階的單位，也就是 cent（分），100 美分就等於 1 美元。所有的美分都是銅板，貨幣符號是 ¢。在美國有 ¢1、¢5、¢10、¢25、¢50 元的銅板，皆有各自的稱呼。

penny [ˋpɛnɪ] 1 分

是最小單位的銅板。

nickel [ˋnɪkəl] 5 分

因為含有金屬鎳（nickel），因此有這樣的別稱。

dime [daɪm] 10 分

是尺寸最小的銅板，比 1 分還要小。

quarter [ˋkwɔrtɚ] 25 分

原本 quarter 是 1/4 的意思，1 元（100 分）的 1/4 就是 25 分，因而得名。

half [hæf] 50 分

half 是「對半」的意思，因為 1 元的一半就是 50 分，所以有這樣的稱號。由於通常是作為紀念幣發行，一般很少見到這種銅板。

觀光時

20 旅遊諮詢處

21 劇院

22 博物館

20 旅遊諮詢處

◎ 請聽以下對話，並跟著說說看。 20-1

對話A

秀智 **Can you recommend** an interesting museum?

[kæn ju ˌrɛkəˋmɛnd æn ˋɪntərɪstɪŋ mjuˋzɪəm]

職員 I'd recommend the Met.

[aɪd ˌrɛkəˋmɛnd ðə mɛt]

對話B

振洙 **Are there any** tours?

[ɑr ðɛr ˋɛnɪ tʊrz]

職員 Yes. Here are some brochures.

[jɛs] [hɪr ɑr sʌm broˋʃʊrz]

句型 39 **Can you recommend + 推薦事物 ?**

你可以推薦～嗎？

「Can you＋動詞?」是藉由詢問「你可以～嗎？」，來拜託其他人某件事情時使用的句子；recommend 則是意為「推薦」的動詞。這是在各種情況下都可以使用的句型，例如：想請人推薦觀光景點或名勝古蹟、在餐廳想請人推薦食物、逛街時想請人推薦不錯的商品時等。

句型 39 你可以推薦有趣的博物館嗎？

句型 40 有（任何）遊覽行程嗎？

20-1

◎ 去一趟旅遊服務中心，可以獲得從有名的觀光景點到美食等有用的旅遊情報。一起來學習要在旅遊服務中心取得資訊時，可以使用的各種表達方式吧！

對話 A

秀智 你可以推薦有趣的博物館嗎？

職員 我推薦大都會（藝術）博物館。

對話 B

振洙 有（任何）遊覽行程嗎？

職員 有的，這裡有些介紹手冊。

新出現的單字

interesting [`ɪntərɪstɪŋ] 有趣的

museum [mju`zɪəm] 博物館

Met [mɛt] 大都會（藝術）博物館

tour [tʊr] 旅遊、觀光

brochure [bro`ʃʊr] 介紹手冊

Met 是指位在美國紐約的 Metropolitan Museum of Art（大都會[藝術]博物館）的縮寫，展示了從古代到現代的各種藝術品。

句型 40 Are there any + 活動 ? 有（任何）～嗎？

Are there ~? 表示「有～嗎？」，和句型 18 的 Is there ~? 具有相同的意義，不過這裡後面所接的單字要使用複數型，像 tours 一樣加上 s 或 es。any 是「任何的、若干」的意思，可以放在名詞前面。Are there any~? 雖然直譯是「有任何～嗎？」的意思，不過解釋成「有～嗎？」也很自然。

句型39 練習

你可以推薦～嗎？

20-2

請將單字帶入空格內並說說看。 20-2

Can you recommend ______?

你可以推薦 ______ 嗎？

a good musical
[ə gʊd `mjuzɪkəl]
不錯的音樂劇

a famous restaurant
[ə `feməs `rɛstərənt]
有名的餐廳

some tourist attractions[1]
[sʌm `tʊrɪst ə`trækʃənz]
一些觀光景點

a nice hotel
[ə naɪs ho`tɛl]
好的飯店

1 some tourist attractions tourist [`tʊrɪst] 是「觀光客、觀光的」，attraction [ə`trækʃən] 則是「（吸引人的）景點」，因此兩個單字組合起來，就形成了「觀光景點」的意思。例如，可視為是紐約象徵的 Statue of Liberty [`stætʃʊ ɑv `lɪbətɪ]（自由女神像）、倫敦的金色鐘塔 Big Ben [bɪg bɛn]（大笨鐘）、可以一眼望盡巴黎都市全景的 Eiffel Tower [`aɪfəl `taʊə]（巴黎鐵塔）等地，都是深具代表性的 tourist attractions。

有（任何）～嗎？

20-3

請將單字帶入空格內並說說看。 20-3

Are there any ______?

有（任何）______嗎？

city tours
[ˋsɪtɪ tʊrz]
城市遊覽行程

night tours
[naɪt tʊrz]
夜間遊覽行程

sporting events[1]
[ˋsportɪŋ ɪˋvɛnts]
運動賽事

local festivals
[ˋlokəl ˋfɛstəvəlz]
地方節慶

1 sporting events sporting 是「運動的」，event 則是「活動、（比賽）項目」的意思。在外國受到歡迎的運動項目有 football [ˋfʊtˏbɔl]「美式足球」、soccer [ˋsɑkɚ]「足球」、baseball [ˋbesˏbɔl]「棒球」、basketball [ˋbæskɪtˏbɔl]「籃球」等等。如果到美國旅遊的話，在以能看見大海聞名的舊金山 AT & T Park 看棒球比賽很不錯；如果是在義大利或西班牙，就好好享受像 AC 米蘭或巴塞隆納足球俱樂部等足球強隊的比賽吧。

對話 觀光之前一定要蒐集情報

20-4

◎ 請聽以下對話，並跟著說說看。 20-4

振洙在正式開始觀光之前，為了得到旅遊資訊而去了趟旅遊服務中心。

振洙 Hello. I'd like to get a city map.
[hə`lo ] [ aɪd laɪk tu gɛt ə `sɪtɪ mæp]

職員 Here you are.
[hɪr ju ɑr]

振洙 **Can you recommend an interesting museum?**
[kæn ju ˏrɛkə`mɛnd æn `ɪntərɪstɪŋ mju`zɪəm]

職員 The Brooklyn Museum is near here, but it's closed today.
[ðə `brʊklɪn mju`zɪəm ɪz nɪr hɪr bʌt ɪts klozd tə`de]

振洙 Then, **are there any tours?**
[ðɛn ɑr ðɛr `ɛnɪ tʊrz]

職員 Yes. You can find brochures on tours over there.
[jɛs] [ju kæn faɪnd bro`ʃʊrz ɑn tʊrz `ovɚ ðɛr]

振洙 Thank you for your help.
[θæŋk ju fɔr jʊɚ hɛlp]

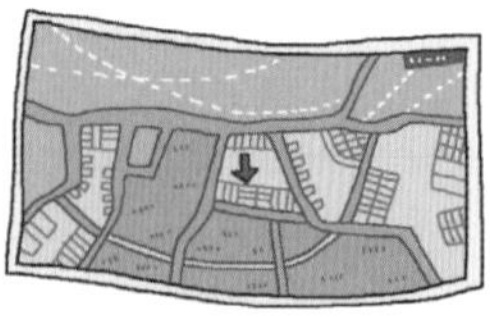

振洙 你好。我想拿張市區地圖。
職員 在這裡。
振洙 **你可以推薦有趣的博物館嗎？**
職員 布魯克林博物館就在附近，不過它今天沒開。
振洙 那麼，**有（任何）遊覽行程嗎？**
職員 有的。你可以在那邊找到與遊覽行程有關的介紹手冊。
振洙 謝謝你的幫忙。

驗收 20 旅遊諮詢處

解答在 221 頁

A 請從選項中選出能填入空格的單字。

選項 **brochures** | **recommend** | **tours** | **museum**

① 你可以推薦有趣的博物館嗎？

Can you ______ an interesting ______?

② 有（任何）遊覽行程嗎？

Are there any ______?

③ 這裡有些介紹手冊。

Here are some ______.

B 請在選項中找出適當的表達方式，並完成下列句子。

選項 **a nice hotel** | **local festivals** | **a famous restaurant** | **city tours**

① 你可以推薦有名的餐廳嗎？

Can you recommend ______?

② 你可以推薦好的飯店嗎？

Can you recommend ______?

③ 有（任何）地方節慶嗎？

Are there any ______?

④ 有（任何）城市遊覽行程嗎？

Are there any ______?

21 劇院

◎ 請聽以下對話，並跟著說說看。 21-1

對話A

售票員 How can I help you?
[haʊ kæn aɪ hɛlp ju]

振洙 **One ticket for *Cats*, please.**
[wʌn ˋtɪkɪt fɔr kæts pliz]

對話B

秀智 **What time does the** show **start**?
[hwɑt taɪm dʌz ðə ʃo stɑrt]

售票員 At 2 o'clock.
[æt tu əˋklɑk]

句型 41 One ticket for + 表演名稱 , please.

（請給我）一張～的票，謝謝。

在劇院或電影院要買票時，只要運用客氣地請託時說的 please 就可以了。One ticket 是「一張票」的意思，如果需要兩張以上的票的時候，請使用「數字（Two, Three, Four...）＋tickets」，如 Two tickets for *Cats* , please.（請給我兩張《貓》的票）來表達。

句型 41 （請給我）一張《貓》的票，謝謝。

句型 42 表演幾點開始？

21-1

到了紐約百老匯或倫敦西區，就可以觀賞世界著名的戲劇表演。一起來學習購買戲票、詢問開演時間的表達方式吧！

對話 A

售票員 需要什麼幫忙嗎？

振洙 （請給我）一張《貓》的票，謝謝。

對話 B

秀智 表演幾點開始？

售票員 2 點整。

新出現的單字

ticket [`tɪkɪt] 票

cat [kæt] 貓

show [ʃo] 表演

start [stɑrt] 開始

o'clock [ə`klɑk] ～點整

Cats 是「貓咪們」的意思，音樂劇《Cats》是講述為了慶典而聚集在一起的貓咪的故事。表演中會有裝扮成貓咪的演員，出沒在觀眾席的各處。

句型 42 What time does the + 表演 + start?

～幾點開始？

這個句型不僅可用來問表演的開始時間，還可以詢問電影、慶典、觀光行程等的開始時間。What time 是「幾點」，start 則是「開始」。另外，如果想知道表演的結束時間，只要將 start（開始）換成 finish [`fɪnɪʃ]（結束）或 end [ɛnd]（結束）來問就可以了。

句型41 練習

（請給我）一張～的票，謝謝。

21-2

請將單字帶入空格內並說說看。 21-2

One ticket for ____, please.

（請給我）一張 ____ 的票，謝謝。

The Lion King[1]

[ðə ˋlaɪən kɪŋ]

《獅子王》

Jekyll and Hyde

[ˋdʒɛkəl ænd haɪd]

《變身怪醫》

Les Misérables[2]

[lɛ ˌmɪzəˈrɑbəl]

《悲慘世界》

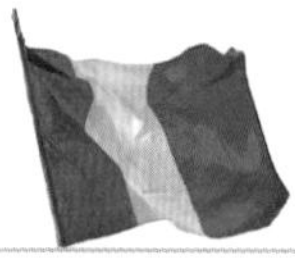

The Phantom of the Opera

[ðə ˋfæntəm ɑv ði ˋɑpərə]

《歌劇魅影》

1 **The Lion King** 根據迪士尼動畫所改編的音樂劇，lion 是「獅子」，king 是「王」的意思。因演員全都以動物裝扮登臺演出而聞名。

2 **Les Misérables** 法文原意是「悲慘的人們」，是改編自維克多・雨果小說的音樂劇。這是世界上演出期間最長的音樂劇，在 2012 年也發行了同名電影。

句型42 練習

～幾點開始？

21-3

◎ 請將單字帶入空格內並說說看。 21-3

What time does the ＿＿＿ start?

＿＿＿幾點開始？

movie
[`muvɪ]
電影

opera[1]
[`ɑpərə]
歌劇

musical
[`mjuzɪkəl]
音樂劇

play
[ple]
舞台劇

ballet[2]
[bæ`le]
芭蕾舞

concert
[`kɑnsɚt]
音樂會、演唱會

1 opera 歌劇主要以文學作品、歷史或神話人物的故事為背景演出。與音樂劇不同，沒有口說的台詞，全劇以歌唱進行表演。歌劇院中以澳洲的 Sydney Opera House [`sɪdnɪ `ɑpərə haʊs]「雪梨歌劇院」特別有名。

2 ballet 芭蕾是僅以舞蹈表現主題與故事的表演，因為沒有台詞，只靠著身體動作來敘述故事，所以就算不懂外語也可以觀賞。

對話 在發源地欣賞原汁原味的表演

21-4

◎ 請聽以下對話，並跟著說說看。 21-4

今天決定要優雅地欣賞表演的秀智，為了買音樂劇門票而去了售票處。

秀智 **One ticket for** *Cats*, **please.**
[wʌn ˋtɪkɪt fɔr kæts pliz]

售票員 For which time? There is a matinee and an evening performance today.
[fɔr hwɪtʃ taɪm] [ðɛr ɪz ə ˋmætənˏe ænd æn ˋivənɪŋ pəˋfɔrməns təˋde]

matinee 日場（午後）表演

秀智 **What time does the show start** in the evening?
[hwɑt taɪm dʌz ðə ʃo stɑrt ɪn ði ˋivənɪŋ]

售票員 It starts at 8.
[ɪt stɑrts æt et]

秀智 Then, I'd like a ticket for the evening performance.
[ðɛn aɪd laɪk ə ˋtɪkɪt fɔr ði ˋivənɪŋ pəˋfɔrməns]

售票員 Okay. Where would you like to sit?
[ˏoˋke] [hwɛr wʊd ju laɪk tu sɪt]

秀智 Can I sit near the front?
[kæn aɪ sɪt nɪr ðə frʌnt]

front 前面

售票員 Yes. Front-row tickets are 40 dollars.
[jɛs] [ˋfrʌntˏro ˋtɪkɪts ɑr ˋfɔrtɪ ˋdɑləz]

秀智 **請給我一張《貓》的票。**
售票員 要幾點的？今天有一場日場和一場晚場表演。
秀智 晚上的**表演幾點開始**？
售票員 8 點開始。
秀智 那麼，請給我晚場表演的票。
售票員 我知道了，你要坐哪裡？
秀智 我可以坐靠前（的位子）嗎？
售票員 可以。前排座位是 40 美金。

驗收 21 劇院

解答在 222 頁

A 請從選項中選出能填入空格的單字。

選項 **o'clock** | **start** | **ticket** | **time**

① （請給我）一張《貓》的票，謝謝。

One ______ for *Cats*, please.

② 表演幾點開始？

What ______ does the show ______?

③ 2 點整。

At 2 ______.

B 請在選項中找出適當的表達方式，並完成下列句子。

選項 **concert** | ***The Lion King*** | **musical** | ***Jekyll and Hyde***

① （請給我）一張《變身怪醫》的票，謝謝。

One ticket for ______, please.

② （請給我）一張《獅子王》的票，謝謝。

One ticket for ______, please.

③ 音樂劇幾點開始？

What time does the ______ start?

④ 音樂會／演唱會幾點開始？

What time does the ______ start?

22 博物館

◎ 請聽以下對話，並跟著說說看。 22-1

對話A

秀智 **What time does the** museum
[hwɑt taɪm dʌz ðə mju`zɪəm

close today?
kloz tə`de]

職員 It closes at 5.
[ɪt klozɪz æt faɪv]

對話B

振洙 **Where can I** get a map of the museum?
[hwɛr kæn aɪ gɛt ə mæp ɑv ðə mju`zɪəm]

職員 You can get one at the front desk.
[ju kæn gɛt wʌn æt ðə frʌnt dɛsk]

句型 43 **What time does the + 地點 + close today?**
今天～幾點關門？

這裡延伸運用句型 42 的 What time（幾點），加上意為「關閉」的動詞 close，可用來詢問包括博物館在內的觀光景點、商店、餐廳等特定場所的關閉、打烊時間。另外，如果好奇開放時間的話，只要以 open [`opən]「開放、營業」取代 close 就可以了。

句型 43 今天博物館幾點關閉？

句型 44 我可以在哪裡拿到博物館地圖？

22-1

在旅途中，會造訪包含博物館和美術館等各式各樣的觀光景點。以博物館為例，來學習可以在各觀光景點使用的句型吧！

對話A

秀智　今天博物館幾點關閉？

職員　5 點關門。

對話B

振洙　我可以在哪裡拿到博物館地圖？

職員　你可以在服務台拿到。

新出現的單字

museum [mju`zɪəm] 博物館

close [kloz] 關閉

today [tə`de] 今天

map [mæp] 地圖

front desk [frʌnt dɛsk] 服務台

front 是「前面」，desk 則是「桌子」。front desk 是指在博物館或飯店等建築物入口處的服務台。

句型 44 Where can I + 動詞 ? 我可以在哪裡～？

Where 是「在哪裡」，can I 是「我可以～嗎？」。構成問句「Where can I＋動詞?」後，意思是「我可以在哪裡～？」，即詢問可以做某行為的地點的句型。經常搭配動詞 get [gɛt]「得到」和 find [faɪnd]「找到」，形成 Where can I get~?（我可以在哪裡拿到～？）和 Where can I find~?（我可以在哪裡找到～？）的句子來使用。

句型43 練習

今天～幾點關閉？

22-2

請將單字帶入空格內並說說看。 22-2

What time does the ______ close today?

今天 ______ 幾點關閉？

palace
[`pælɪs]
宮殿

zoo
[zu]
動物園

aquarium
[ə`kwɛrɪəm]
水族館

cathedral[1]
[kə`θidrəl]
大教堂

art museum
[ɑrt mju`zɪəm]
美術館

botanical garden[2]
[bo`tænɪkəl `gɑrdən]
植物園

1 cathedral 這是在歐洲歷史悠久、規模龐大的教堂附近，經常能看到的單字。依巴洛克風格建造的倫敦 St. Paul's Cathedral [sent pɔlz kə`θidrəl]（聖保羅大教堂）相當有名，台灣的前金天主堂也屬於 cathedral。

2 botanical garden botanical 是「植物的」，garden 則是「花園」，因此 botanical garden 就是植物園。美國的 New York botanical garden [nju jɔrk bo`tænɪkəl `gɑrdən]（紐約植物園）特別地著名。

我可以在哪裡～？

22-3

◎ 請將單字帶入空格內並說說看。 22-3

Where can I ______?

我可以在哪裡 ______？

buy a ticket
[baɪ ə ˋtɪkɪt]
買票

find the restroom
[faɪnd ðə ˋrɛstˏrum]
找到廁所

rent an audio guide[1]
[rɛnt æn ˋɔdɪˏo gaɪd]
租借語音導覽

get a brochure[2]
[gɛt ə broˋʃʊr]
拿到介紹手冊

1 **rent an audio guide** rent 是「租借」，audio 是「聲音的」，guide 則是「指引、導遊；指南」，audio guide 是指在博物館或展覽會場，提供給觀展客人的「語音導覽器」。由長得像手機一般的機器和耳機組成，可以隨身攜帶，以聽取與博物館展品相關的介紹。

2 **get a brochure** brochure 是從法文而來的單字，意思是做得輕薄、提供資訊用的小手冊。更薄的手冊則稱為 pamphlet [ˋpæmflɪt]。

對話 今天要有文化地參觀博物館

22-4

請聽以下對話，並跟著說說看。 22-4

下午較晚抵達博物館的振洙，為了買票去了售票處。

振洙 **What time does the museum close today?**
[hwɑt taɪm dʌz ðə mju`zɪəm kloz tə`de]

職員 It closes at 6 on Mondays. **Monday** 星期一
[ɪt klozɪz æt sɪks ɑn `mʌndez]

振洙 What's the admission fee? **admission fee** 入場費用
[hwɑts ði əd`mɪʃən fi]

職員 It's 16 dollars for adults. **adult** 成人、大人
[ɪts `sɪks͵tin `dɑlɚz fɔr ə`dʌlts]

振洙 Okay. One adult, please.
[͵o`ke ] [ wʌn ə`dʌlt pliz]

職員 Here's your ticket.
[hirz jʊɚ `tɪkɪt]

振洙 **Where can I get a map of the museum?**
[hwɛr kæn aɪ gɛt ə mæp ɑv ðə mju`zɪəm]

職員 You can get a free map at the entrance. **entrance** 入口
[ju kæn gɛt ə fri mæp æt ði `ɛntrəns]

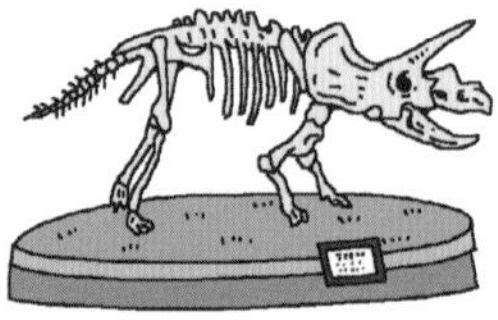

振洙 **今天博物館幾點關閉？**
職員 星期一都是 6 點關。
振洙 入場費用多少錢呢？
職員 成人是 16 美金。
振洙 好的。（請給我）一張成人票，謝謝。
職員 你的票在這裡。
振洙 **我可以在哪裡拿到博物館地圖？**
職員 你可以在入口處拿到免費地圖。

驗收 22 博物館

解答在 222 頁

A 請從選項中選出能填入空格的單字。

選項 **front** | **map** | **time** | **close**

① 今天博物館幾點關閉？

What ______ does the museum ______ today?

② 我可以在哪裡拿到博物館地圖？

Where can I get a ______ of the museum?

③ 你可以在服務台拿到。

You can get one at the ______ desk.

B 請在選項中找出適當的表達方式，並完成下列句子。

選項 **get a brochure** | **buy a ticket** | **zoo** | **art museum**

① 今天美術館幾點關閉？

What time does the ______ close today?

② 今天動物園幾點關閉？

What time does the ______ close today?

③ 我可以在哪裡買票？

Where can I ______?

④ 我可以在哪裡拿到介紹手冊？

Where can I ______?

Tourist information 旅客資訊中心

tourist 是「觀光客、旅客」，information 是「資訊」的意思，而 tourist information [`tʊrɪst ˌɪnfɚ`meʃən] 則是表示觀光客能夠獲得各種資訊的諮詢處，其標誌也會用這個詞組，或者是取 information 的頭文字 i 來標示。

Lost and Found 失物招領處

Lost and Found [lɔst ænd faʊnd] 是由 lost（遺失的、丟失的）和 found（被發現的）兩個字組成，表示遺失物保管處，是經常在博物館或遊樂園裡看見的設施標誌。

Tickets 票

ticket 是「票、入場券」的意思，在觀光景點看到標誌上寫有 Tickets，就是指販售票券的售票處。另外，劇院或電影院的售票處則稱為 box office [bɑks `ɔfɪs]。

Sold out 售完

sold out [sold aʊt] 表示「售完的、缺貨的」，是表演的票售罄時會看到的標誌，也可以表示商店內物品都賣光、沒有了的意思。

General admission 一般入場費

admission 意為「入場費用」，general 則是「一般的」。博物館多半會給 Child [tʃaɪld]（孩童）、Senior [`sinjɚ]（年長者）及 Student [`stjudənt]（學生）入場費優惠。general admission [`dʒɛnərəl əd`mɪʃən] 則是指一般成人所要付的「一般入場費」。

No photography 禁止攝影

No 也能用來表示「禁止」，而 photography [fə`tɑgrəfɪ] 則表示「拍照」，合在一起就是「禁止拍照攝影」的意思。有時也會簡單地以意為「禁止照片」的 No Photos [no `fotoz] 或 No pictures [no `pɪktʃɚz] 來標示。

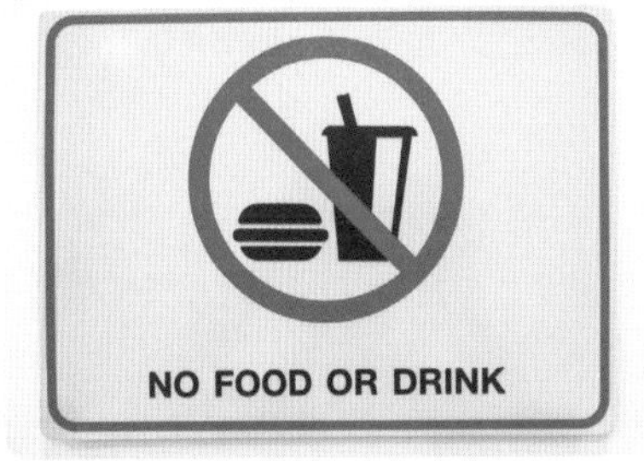

No food or drink 禁止飲食

food 是「食物」，drink 則是「飲料」，合在一起變成「禁止食物或飲料」，也就是「場內禁止飲食」的意思。為了防止展示品或設備毀損，包含博物館在內，有許多不能帶食物進入的地方，所以請多留意這個標誌。

Silence please 請保持安靜

silence [`saɪləns] 是代表「安靜、沉默」，也有「肅靜」的意思。後面加上 please，就是表示「請保持安靜」的標誌。是在展覽廳、劇院或動物園等地很常見的句型。

生動的旅遊情報

歡度節日

到國外旅遊時，
度過那個國家的節日，
也是感受當地人
生活的好方法。
來認識西方國家的
代表性節日吧！

Thanksgiving Day 感恩節

Thanksgiving Day [ˌθæŋksˋgɪvɪŋ de] 是與中秋節類似的傳統節日，美國訂在 11 月的第四個星期四，加拿大則訂在 10 月的第二個星期一。感恩節是家人團聚的日子，大家會一起做料理，享用火雞和玉米等食物。在美國感恩節隔天的星期五，被稱為 Black Friday（黑色星期五），許多店家會祭出折扣活動，是購物的最佳時機。

Christmas 聖誕節

Christmas [ˋkrɪsməs] 聖誕節（12月25日）在西方國家是相當重大的節日，和感恩節一樣都是家族團聚的日子。特別是從 11 月月底到聖誕節的這段時間被稱為「聖誕季」，在德國和奧地利等歐洲各國的廣場，會舉辦傳統的聖誕市集，可以在這裡買到各種聖誕節的裝飾品，還有起司、紅酒等各式各樣的食品。

Halloween 萬聖節

Halloween [ˌhæloˋin] 是愛爾蘭移民帶來的節日，在 10 月 31 日慶祝。孩子會打扮成怪物和幽靈的模樣，挨家挨戶地討糖果，成人也會盛裝打扮參與派對，住家附近也會以南瓜做的燈、幽靈或蜘蛛網模型來裝飾。美國的商家從 10 月開始進入萬聖節季，會販賣萬聖節的服裝、道具及裝飾品等各種物品，如果想買到特別的紀念品，請把握這個時機。

New Year’s Day 元旦

1 月 1 日是 New Year’s Day [nju jɪrz de]，世界各地從前天晚上開始，舉辦盛大的慶典，尤其 12 月 31 日晚上，在紐約時代廣場會展開世界知名歌手的演出。也有在跨年倒數到零，正式進入新的一年之際，整晚吊掛在空中的球向下掉落這樣有趣的活動，會有眾多人潮聚在一起慶祝新年。

發生問題時

23 找路

24 失竊報案

23 找路

◎ 請聽以下對話，並跟著說說看。 23-1

對話A

振洙 **How can I get to** Central Park?

[haʊ kæn aɪ gɛt tu `sɛntrəl pɑrk]

路人 Take the number 5 bus.

[tek ðə `nʌmbɚ faɪv bʌs]

對話B

秀智 **Where is the nearest** bus stop?

[hwɛr ɪz ðə nɪrɪst bʌs stɑp]

路人 Go straight and turn left at the corner.

[go stret ænd tɝn lɛft æt ðə `kɔrnɚ]

句型 45 How can I get to + 地點 ? 我要怎麼去～？

這是在詢問該怎麼去某個地點時，可以使用的句型。how 是「如何」的意思，是用來詢問方法或手段的疑問詞。「How can I＋動詞」表示「我該怎麼樣才能～？」，get to（抵達）後面可以帶入各種地點，以詢問到達該地點的交通方式，或是走過去的路徑。

句型 45 我要怎麼去中央公園？
句型 46 最近的公車站牌在哪裡？

23-1

旅行途中如果因為迷路而徬徨時，請不要猶豫，向當地人詢問吧！現在就來學學在這種情況下，該如何用英語來問路。

對話 A

振洙 我要怎麼去中央公園？

職員 搭 5 號公車。

對話 B

秀智 最近的公車站牌在哪裡？

職員 直走後在街角左轉。

新出現的單字

get to [gɛt tu] 抵達～

park [pɑrk] 公園

bus stop [bʌs stɑp] 公車站牌

go [go] 去

straight [stret] 徑直、一直

turn [tɝn] 轉、拐彎

left [lɛft] 往左、左邊

corner [ˋkɔrnɚ] 街角、轉角

句型 46 Where is the nearest + 地點 ? 最近的～在哪裡？

這是在問路時最具代表性的句子。如同前面所學過的，Where is ~? 是詢問地點的句型，the nearest 表示「最近的」，是形容詞 near（近的）加上了 -est 的最高級形式。要詢問離自己現在位置最近的某個地點時，請運用這個句型。

句型45 練習　我要怎麼去～？

23-2

◎ 請將單字帶入空格內並說說看。 23-2

How can I get to ☐?

我要怎麼去 ☐？

the Korean embassy

[ðə ko`riən `ɛmbəsɪ]

韓國大使館

the natural history museum[1]

[ðə `nætʃərəl `hɪstərɪ mju`zɪəm]

自然史博物館

Liberty Island[2]

[`lɪbə-tɪ `aɪlənd]

自由島

Queen's Theater

[`kwinz `θɪətə-]

皇后劇院

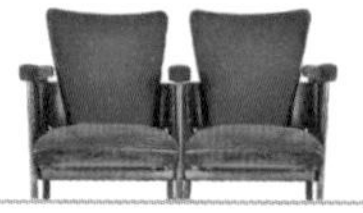

1 **the natural history museum**　natural 是「自然的」，history 是「歷史」，museum 則是「博物館」。natural history museum 如同字面上的意思，就是指展示了動植物、地質等與大自然歷史相關資料的博物館。

2 **Liberty Island**　liberty 是「自由」，island 則是「島」，自由島是 Statue of Liberty [`stætʃʊ ɑv `lɪbə-tɪ]「自由女神像」所在的小島，位在美國紐約，可以搭免費的渡船前往。

最近的～在哪裡？

23-3

請將單字帶入空格內並說說看。 23-3

Where is the nearest ______?

最近的 ______ 在哪裡？

taxi stand
[ˋtæksɪ stænd]
計程車招呼站

subway station
[ˋsʌbˏwe ˋsteʃən]
地鐵站

supermarket
[ˋsupɚˏmarkɪt]
超級市場

department store[1]
[dɪˋpartmənt stor]
百貨公司

■ **多樣的場所** 請帶入 gas station [gæs ˋsteʃən]「加油站」、convenience store [kənˋvinjəns stor]「便利商店」、coffee shop [ˋkɔfɪ ʃɑp]「咖啡廳」、fast food restaurant [fæst fud ˋrɛstərənt]「速食餐廳」等各種地點，來詢問附近是否有這些場所吧！

1 department store department 是意為「部門、（商場中的各個）賣場」的單字，因為百貨公司是由許多個賣場所組成的一間商店（store），因此稱為 department store。

對話 問著問著找公園

23-4

請聽以下對話，並跟著說說看。 23-4

身為路痴的秀智正因為迷路而徬徨不已，最後她決定向別人問路。

秀智 Excuse me. **How can I get to Central Park?**
[ɪk`skjuz mi ] [ haʊ kæn aɪ gɛt tu `sɛntrəl park]

路人 It's quite far from here. quite 相當
[ɪts kwaɪt fɑr frɑm hɪr]

秀智 How far is it? far 遠的
[haʊ fɑr ɪz ɪt]

路人 It takes 30 minutes on foot. on foot 徒步
[ɪt teks `θɝtɪ `mɪnɪts ɑn fʊt]

It's better to take the bus. better 較好的
[ɪts `bɛtɚ tu tek ðə bʌs]

秀智 **Where is the nearest bus stop?**
[hwɛr ɪz ðə nɪrɪst bʌs stɑp]

路人 Go straight and turn right at the bookstore. right 右邊
[go stret ænd tɝn raɪt æt ðə `bʊk͵stor] bookstore 書店

Take the number 5 bus.
[tek ðə `nʌmbɚ faɪv bʌs]

秀智 不好意思，**我要怎麼去中央公園？**
路人 那距離這裡滿遠的。
秀智 多遠？
路人 走路要花 30 分鐘。搭公車比較好。
秀智 **最近的公車站牌在哪裡？**
路人 直走，並在書店右轉。搭 5 號公車。

驗收 23 找路

解答在 222 頁

A 請從選項中選出能填入空格的單字。

選項 **straight** | **get** | **corner** | **nearest**

① 我要怎麼去中央公園？

How can I ______ to Central Park?

② 最近的公車站牌在哪裡？

Where is the ______ bus stop?

③ 直走後在街角左轉。

Go ______ and turn left at the ______.

B 請在選項中找出適當的表達方式，並完成下列句子。

選項 **Liberty Island** | **the Korean embassy** | **subway station** | **department store**

① 我要怎麼去韓國大使館？

How can I get to ______?

② 我要怎麼去自由島？

How can I get to ______?

③ 最近的百貨公司在哪裡？

Where is the nearest ______?

④ 最近的地鐵站在哪裡？

Where is the nearest ______?

24 失竊報案

◎ 請聽以下對話，並跟著說說看。 24-1

對話A

振洙 **Is there a** police station **around here**?
[ɪz ðɛr ə pə`lis `steʃən ə`raʊnd hɪr]

行人 Yes. There's one across the street.
[jɛs] [ðɛrz wʌn ə`krɔs ðə strit]

對話B

警察 How can I help you?
[haʊ kæn aɪ hɛlp ju]

秀智 **My** bag **was stolen**.
[maɪ bæg wɑz `stolən]

句型 47 Is there a [an] + 場所 +around here?

這附近有～嗎？

這是詢問附近是否有某個場所時可以使用的句型。「Is there＋名詞」是「有～嗎？」的意思，around here 則是「在這附近」。請注意，如果是詢問任一間警察局，而不是特指某分局時，場所前面不加 the，而是加上 a 或是 an。除了 around here 之外，也可以使用相同意思的 near here [nɪr hɪr]。

句型 47 **這附近有警察局嗎？**

句型 48 **我的包包被偷了。**

24-1

在旅行途中，沒有什麼事比東西被偷更令人感到困擾了。來學物品遭竊，或發生緊急狀況時能夠應對的表達方式吧！

對話A

振洙 這附近有警察局嗎？

行人 有。對街有一間。

對話B

警察 有什麼我能幫助你的嗎？

秀智 我的包包被偷了。

新出現的單字

police station [pə`lis `steʃən] 警察局

around here [ə`raʊnd hɪr] 在附近

across [ə`krɔs] 對面

street [strit] 街道

stolen [`stolən] 遭竊的

句型 48 **My + 物品 + was stolen.** 我的～被偷了。

stolen 是 steal [stil]「偷竊、竊盜」的過去分詞，可作為形容詞使用，意思是「被偷的、遭竊的」。物品遭竊的事實與自己講述的當下相比，已經是過去，因此必須要使用過去式 was stolen 來表達。同理，物品遺失時，也要以 lose [luz]「遺失」的過去式 lost [lɔst]「遺失了」，構成「I lost my＋物品.」來表達。

句型47 練習

這附近有～嗎？

24-2

請將單字帶入空格內並說說看。 24-2

Is there a ______ around here?

這附近有 ______ 嗎？

hospital
[ˋhɑspɪtəl]
醫院

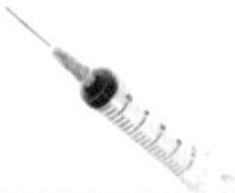

drugstore[1]
[ˋdrʌgˏstor]
藥妝店

restroom
[ˋrɛstˏrum]
洗手間

bank
[bæŋk]
銀行

post office
[post ˋɔfɪs]
郵局

pay phone[2]
[pe fon]
公共電話

1 **drugstore** 是不用處方箋就能購買的藥品，並同時販售維他命、化妝品等商品的商店。須以處方箋向藥師提領藥品的「藥局」則是 pharmacy [ˋfɑrməsɪ]。

2 **pay phone** pay 是「支付」，phone 是「電話」的意思，合在一起就是指用銅板或信用卡付錢使用的「公共電話」。雖然最近因為有手機，幾乎不需要使用公共電話，但是為了應付緊急狀況，還是請記起來。

句型48 練習

我的～被偷了。

24-3

◎ 請將單字帶入空格內並說說看。 24-3

My ______ was stolen.

我的 ______ 被偷了。

wallet
[ˋwɑlɪt]
皮夾

backpack[1]
[ˋbæk͵pæk]
背包

handbag
[ˋhænd͵bæg]
手提包

cellphone[2]
[ˋsɛlfon]
手機

credit card
[ˋkrɛdɪt kɑrd]
信用卡

camera
[ˋkæmərə]
相機

1 backpack back 是「背、後」，pack 是「包、包裹」的意思，backpack 照字面的意思，就是指背在背上的「背包」。

2 cellphone 「手機」用英語表示並不是 handphone，而是 cellphone，是 cellular phone [ˋsɛljulɚ fon] 的縮寫，在英國也稱為 mobile phone [ˋmobaɪl fon]。另外，可以連接網路的智慧型手機則是 smartphone [ˋsmɑrtfon]。

對話 在太遲之前趕快報案

24-4

◎ 請聽以下對話，並跟著說說看。 24-4

小偷偷了秀智的包包之後逃跑了，秀智正急著找警察局。

秀智 Excuse me. **Is there a police station around here?**
[ɪk`skjuz mi ] [ ɪz ðɛr ə pə`lis `steʃən ə`raʊnd hɪr]

行人 Yes, it's just around the corner.
[jɛs ɪts dʒʌst ə`raʊnd ðə `kɔrnɚ]

秀智 Thank you.
[θæŋk ju]

一會兒後，秀智為了要報案而走進了警局。

秀智 Hello. I'd like to report a theft.
[hə`lo ] [ aɪd laɪk tu rɪ`port ə θɛft]

report 報告、檢舉
theft 盜竊、偷盜

警察 Okay. What was stolen?
[ˌo`ke ] [ hwɑt wɑz `stolən]

秀智 **My bag was stolen.**
[maɪ bæg wɑz `stolən]

警察 What was in it?
[hwɑt wɑz ɪn ɪt]

秀智 My camera and passport.
[maɪ `kæmərə ænd `pæsˌport]

秀智 不好意思，**這附近有警察局嗎？**
行人 有，就在附近。
秀智 謝謝。

秀智 你好，我想報案遭竊。
警察 好的。什麼東西被偷了？
秀智 **我的包包被偷了。**
警察 裡面有什麼？
秀智 我的相機和護照。

驗收 24 失竊報案

解答在 223 頁

A 請從選項中選出能填入空格的單字。

選項 **stolen** **around** **across** **police**

① 這附近有警察局嗎？

Is there a ______ station ______ here?

② 有。對街有一間。

Yes. There's one ______ the street.

③ 我的包包被偷了。

My bag was ______.

B 請在選項中找出適當的表達方式，並完成下列句子。

選項 **wallet** **hospital** **cellphone** **bank**

① 這附近有銀行嗎？

Is there a ______ around here?

② 這附近有醫院嗎？

Is there a ______ around here?

③ 我的皮夾被偷了。

My ______ was stolen.

④ 我的手機被偷了。

My ______ was stolen.

24-5

Road 路

road [rod] 是「道路、路」的意思，在地圖或路標上面也會縮寫成 Rd.。相同地，Street [strit]（街）會縮寫成 St., Avenue [`ævə͵nju]（道）是 Av., Boulevard [`bulə͵vɑrd]（大道、林蔭道）則是 Blvd.。

Restroom 洗手間

在美國，洗手間通常被標成 restroom [`rɛst͵rum]，不過在英國則是 toilet [`tɔɪlɪt]。在澳洲或英國也有很多標示成 loo [lu] 的地方。男性洗手間會加上 Men，女性洗手間則會加上 Women。

Keep off 禁止進入

keep off [kip ɔf] 是「遠離～」的意思，就是指「禁止進入」，keep off the grass [græs]「禁止進入草皮」也是在路上常會看到的標誌。keep out [kip aʊt] 也是指「禁止進入」。

Danger 危險

danger [`dendʒɚ] 表示「危險」，是警告標誌上很常見的單字。與此相同，用在警告標誌上的字還有 Caution [`kɔʃən]「注意」和 Warning [`wɔrnɪŋ]「警告」。

No access 禁止通行

access [`æksɛs] 是「接近」的意思，前面如果加上 no 的話，就能用來表示不可以接近、「禁止通行」。另外在 no 和 access 中間加入 pedestrian [pə`dɛstrɪən]「行人」的 No pedestrian access 標誌是「禁止行人通行」的意思。

Do not litter 請勿亂丟垃圾

Do not 是「請勿」的意思，是在禁止標誌上很常見的用字。litter 表示「亂丟」，而 Do not litter [du nɑt `lɪtɚ] 就是「請勿亂丟垃圾」的意思，也會寫成 No littering。

Dead end 此路不通

dead 雖然是指「死亡的」，但是也能表示「無效的、不動的」，end 的意思則是「盡頭」，因此 dead end [dɛd ɛnd] 就是指一端不通的道路或通道等，即「死路」。No outlet [`aʊt͵lɛt]（沒有出口）也是相同的意思，都是標誌上經常使用的字。

One way 單行道

way 有「方向」的意思，因此 one way [wʌn we] 就是表示只能依一個方向前進的「單行道」，是在路上常見的標誌。

生動的旅遊情報

危急時需要的英語

在旅行途中，有時候
會發生緊急狀況。
來認識像台灣的 119 一樣的
緊急電話號碼，
以及藥品和
疾病症狀的單字吧。

各國的緊急救難電話號碼

119 韓國、日本、中國
與台灣一樣，韓國、日本及中國的緊急救難電話號碼也是 119。

112 歐洲國家
義大利、西班牙、法國、德國、比利時、波蘭、葡萄牙、捷克、挪威、丹麥、克羅埃西亞等，通用於大部分的歐洲國家。

911 美國、加拿大、墨西哥

999 英國、卡達、馬來西亞、香港

000 澳洲

111 紐西蘭

117 菲律賓、柬埔寨

115 越南

1669 泰國

醫藥品

pill [pɪl] 藥丸

aspirin [`æspərɪn] 阿斯匹靈

painkiller [`pen͵kɪlɚ] 止痛藥

fever reducer [`fivɚ rɪ`djusɚ] 退燒藥

digestive medicine
[də`dʒɛstɪv `mɛdəsən] 腸胃藥

anti-diarrheal [`æntɪ ͵daɪə`ril] 止瀉藥

cough syrup [kɔf `sɪrəp] 咳嗽糖漿

Band-Aid [`bænd͵ed] ok 繃

bandage [`bændɪdʒ] 繃帶

thermometer [θɚ`mɑmətɚ] 體溫計

疾病症狀

fever [`fivɚ] 發燒

cold [kold] 感冒

headache [`hɛd͵ek] 頭痛

stomachache [`stʌmək͵ek] 胃痛

backache [`bæk͵ek] 背痛

toothache [`tuθ͵ek] 牙痛

earache [`ɪr͵ek] 耳朵痛

cough [kɔf] 咳嗽

runny nose [`rʌnɪ noz] 流鼻水

stuffy nose [`stʌfɪ noz] 鼻塞

sore throat [sor θrot] 喉嚨痛

diarrhea [͵daɪə`riə] 腹瀉

allergy [`ælɚdʒɪ] 過敏

indigestion [͵ɪndə`dʒɛstʃən]
消化不良

回國時

25 登機手續

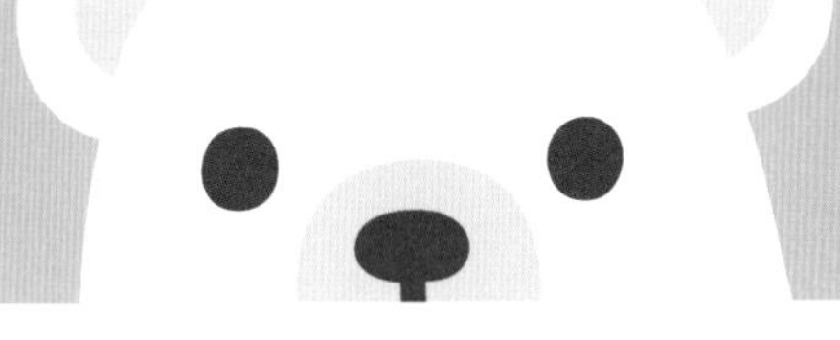

25 登機手續

◎ 請聽以下對話，並跟著說說看。 25-1

對話A

地勤 **Can I see your** passport?

[kæn aɪ si jʊɚ `pæs͵port]

振洙 Here you are.

[hɪr ju ɑr]

對話B

秀智 **Can I have** a window seat?

[kæn aɪ hæv ə `wɪndo sit]

地勤 I'm sorry, but they are all taken.

[aɪm `sɑrɪ bʌt ðe ɑr ɔl `tekən]

句型 49 **Can I see your + 物品 ?** 我可以看看你的～嗎？

這是想確認對方所持物品時使用的問句，在機場經常能從地勤人員或空服員那裡聽到。這裡動詞 see 是「看」，「Can I＋動詞?」是在請託他人某事時說的「我可以～嗎？」。若要更客氣地表示時，也可以說「May I＋動詞?」。

句型 49 我可以看看你的護照嗎？

句型 50 我可以坐靠窗的座位嗎？

25-1

結束了所有的行程，終於到了要回國的日子。來學搭上回國飛機之前，在機場辦理登機手續時使用的表達方式吧！

對話A

地勤 我可以看看你的護照嗎？

振洙 在這裡。

對話B

秀智 我可以坐靠窗的座位嗎？

地勤 不好意思，所有（靠窗）的座位都滿了。

新出現的單字

see [si] 看

passport [ˋpæsˏport] 護照

window [ˋwɪndo] 窗戶

seat [sit] 座位

all [ɔl] 全部

taken [ˋtekən] （座位被）坐了

動詞 take 有「坐（在座位）」的意思，因此過去分詞 taken 就是「（座位）被坐了」的意思。

句型 50 Can I have + 座位種類 ? 我可以坐～嗎？

辦理登機手續時，如果想問是否能坐在特定座位時，請運用 Can I have ~? 的句型。直譯是「我可以有～嗎？」的意思，後面帶入想要的飛機座位種類，就可以詢問「我可以坐～的座位嗎？」。也可以將主詞 I 換成 we，以 Can we have two seats together?（我們可以坐相連的兩個座位嗎？）來提問。

句型49 練習 我可以看看你的～嗎？

25-2

請將單字帶入空格內並說說看。 25-2

Can I see your ______?

我可以看看你的 ______ 嗎？

boarding pass[1]
[ˋbordɪŋ pæs]
登機證

customs form
[ˋkʌstəmz fɔrm]
關稅申報單

driver's license[2]
[ˋdraɪvɚz ˋlaɪsəns]
駕照

ticket
[ˋtɪkɪt]
票

1 **boarding pass** boarding 是「登上、搭上（飛機、巴士等交通工具）」，pass 則是「通行證、交通票」的意思，boarding pass 就是可以搭乘飛機的「登機證」，在航空公司櫃台辦理登機手續時，只要出示紙本或電子機票和護照，就能得到登機證。

句型50 練習

我可以坐～嗎？

25-3

請將單字帶入空格內並說說看。 25-3

Can I have ______?

我可以坐 ______ 嗎？

an aisle seat
[æn aɪl sit]
靠走道的座位

an exit-row seat[1]
[æn `ɛksɪt͵ro sit]
緊急逃生口旁的座位

a first-row seat
[ə `fɝst͵ro sit]
最前排的座位

a seat next to my friend
[ə sit nɛkst tu maɪ frɛnd]
我朋友旁邊的座位

1 an exit-row seat row 是「（座位的）排」，飛機機體中間有緊急降落時使用的緊急出口（exit），exit-row seat 就是在緊急出口旁邊的座位。因為必須在緊急狀況時協助空服人員，所以多是身體健康、通曉英語的人被安排在此。

對話 現在搭飛機回家吧

25-4

請聽以下對話，並跟著說說看。 25-4

旅途的最後一天，抵達機場的振洙為了辦理登機手續而來到航空公司櫃檯。

振洙 I'd like to check in.
[aɪd laɪk tu tʃɛk ɪn]

check in **辦理登機手續**

地勤 **Can I see your passport?**
[kæn aɪ si jʊɚ `pæs,port]

振洙 Here it is.
[hɪr ɪt ɪz]

地勤 Would you like a window seat or an aisle seat?
[wʊd ju laɪk ə `wɪndo sit ɔr æn aɪl sit]

振洙 **Can I have a window seat?**
[kæn aɪ hæv ə `wɪndo sit]

地勤 Yes. How many bags will you be checking?
[jɛs] [haʊ `mɛnɪ bægz wɪl ju bi tʃɛkɪŋ]

振洙 Two.
[tu]

地勤 Put your bags on the scale one at a time, please.
[pʊt jʊɚ bægz ɑn ðə skel wʌn æt ə taɪm pliz]

scale **秤**

振洙 我想辦理登機手續。
地勤 **我可以看看你的護照嗎？**
振洙 在這裡。
地勤 你想坐靠窗還是靠走道的座位？
振洙 **我可以坐靠窗的座位嗎？**
地勤 可以。你要託運幾件行李？
振洙 兩件。
地勤 請將你的行李一次一件放到秤上。

驗收 25 登機手續

解答在 223 頁

A 請從選項中選出能填入空格的單字。

選項 **see** | **taken** | **window** | **passport**

① 我可以坐靠窗的座位嗎？

Can I have a ______ seat?

② 不好意思，所有（靠窗）的座位都滿了。

I'm sorry, but they are all ______.

③ 我可以看看你的護照嗎？

Can I ______ your ______?

B 請在選項中找出適當的表達方式，並完成下列句子。

選項 **boarding pass** | **driver's license**
an aisle seat | **an exit-row seat**

① 我可以看看你的駕照嗎？

Can I see your ______?

② 我可以看看你的登機證嗎？

Can I see your ______?

③ 我可以坐靠走道的座位嗎？

Can I have ______?

④ 我可以坐緊急逃生口旁的座位嗎？

Can I have ______?

25-5

International departures

國際線出境

根據機場的不同，有時候國內線和國際線出發的地點會不同。domestic [dəˋmɛstɪk] 表示「國內的」，international 是「國際的」。出國的話，請跟著 International departures [ˌɪntɚˋnæʃənəl dɪˋpɑrtʃɚz]「國際線出境」的標誌移動。

Terminal 航廈

terminal [ˋtɝmənəl] 是指搭乘及下飛機的建築物。規模較大的機場，會有不同航空公司分別使用不同航廈的情況，最好提早確認要搭乘的班機是在哪個航廈。

Check in 登機手續

在機場 check in [tʃɛk ɪn] 是指「登機手續」，在航空公司的登機櫃台出示護照和紙本或電子機票，領取登機證並託運行李就可以了。最近也可以由乘客自己直接利用機器辦理手續、取得登機證並託運行李。

Security check 安全檢查（安檢）站

security 是「保安、安全」，check 是「檢查、確認」，security check [sɪˋkjʊrətɪ tʃɛk] 是指透過 X 光機檢查行李的「安全檢查（安檢）站」。有些國家在進出購物中心或飯店時，也需經過安全檢查站。

Gate 登機門

gate [get] 是「門、出入口」的意思，在機場則是指登機門。確認寫在登機證上的 gate 號碼後，到登機門附近區域等待搭機就可以了。

Tax refund 退稅

tax 是「稅金」，refund 是「退費」，退稅是以外國人不會在當地使用旅途中所買的物品，並會將該物品帶回自己國家自用為前提，退還所買物品的附加價值稅，而機場的 tax refund [tæks `riˌfʌnd] 正是辦這個手續的地方。

Duty-free 免稅的、免稅品、免稅店

duty 是「稅金」，free 是「自由的、免於～的」，所以 duty-free [`djutɪ fri] 就是「免稅的」，也是指免除稅金的「免稅品」，及販賣這些商品的「免稅店」。只要通過安全檢查站進入航站管制區內後，就可以光顧這些店面。

Delayed 延誤的

只要看機場的電子顯示板，就可以確認航班的出發時間。Delayed [dɪ`led]（延誤的）是指飛機誤點的意思，On time（準時的）則表示飛機將準時於預定時間出發。

生動的旅遊情報

檢視登機證

在機場收到登機證後，
很容易因為所有欄位都是英文
而感到慌張。
雖然每間航空公司的格式略有不同，
但是只要記住以下的內容
就不需要擔心了。

Name 姓名

登機證上所寫的姓名一定要和護照的英文姓名相同，如果不一樣，地勤有可能會拒絕讓你登機，所以請務必要提早確認。

From / To 從～／到～

from 指出出發地點，to 則帶出目的地。雖然也有像 CHICAGO（芝加哥）、LONDON（倫敦）這樣寫出城市名稱的情況，但有時也會以機場的三碼英文縮寫來標記。舉例來說，像桃園國際機場（Taoyuan International Airport）是 TPE，紐約的約翰·甘迺迪國際機場（John F. Kennedy International Airport）則標示為 JFK。

Flight 航班號碼

航班號碼由各航空公司的代碼及數字組成。例如，中華航空公司的代碼是 CI，長榮航空公司的代碼則是 BR，代碼後面加上數字，就會形成如 BR-282、CI161 等的航班號碼。

Class 艙等

登機證上有時候會以 economy（經濟艙）、business（商務艙）、first（頭等艙）這些字來表示機艙內座位的等級。

Seat 座位

座位號碼由英文字母和數字所組成，可以看著登機證上寫的 Seat 欄位來尋找自己在飛機內的座位。

Boarding time 登機時間

飛機登機時間通常比出發時間早 20 到 30 分鐘左右開放。務必確認登機時間，不要太晚到自己的登機口，以免遲到。

Gate 登機門

登機證上所寫的登機門，有時候也會變更。因此最好經常查看機場內的電子顯示板，以確認是否有變動。

確認看看

各單元〈驗收〉的正確答案

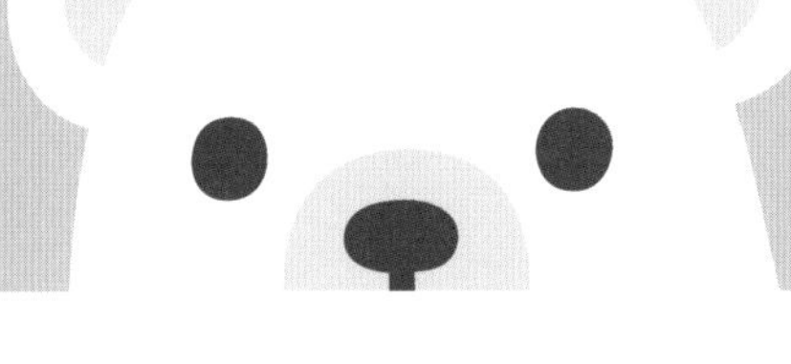

01 飛機餐 31 頁

A ① Would you like something to drink ?
② Chicken or beef?
③ Beef, please .

B ① Would you like some water ?
② Would you like a glass of wine ?
③ Coke , please.
④ Fish , please.

02 機內服務 37 頁

A ① Can I get a blanket?
② Sure .
③ Could you take my tray ?

B ① Can I get a newspaper ?
② Can I get headphones ?
③ Could you wake me for meals ?
④ Could you switch seats with me ?

03 入境審查 47 頁

A ① I'm here for sightseeing .
② I plan to stay for ten days.
③ What is the purpose of your visit?

B ① I'm here to visit my friend .

② I'm here on vacation .

③ I plan to stay for a week .

④ I plan to stay for about ten days .

領取行李

53 頁

A ① What's your flight number ?

② Do you have your baggage claim ticket?

③ Here you are.

B ① What's your name ?

② What's your home address ?

③ Do you have any liquids ?

④ Do you have anything to declare ?

公車

63 頁

A ① Which bus goes to Times Square?

② Does this bus go to Times Square?

③ You should take the number 10 bus.

B ① Which bus goes to Victoria Station ?

② Which bus goes to the baseball stadium ?

③ Does this bus go to Fifth Avenue ?

④ Does this bus go to City Hall ?

06 計程車 69 頁

A ① How long does it take to get to the hotel?
② Could you take me to the Sun Hotel?
③ It takes about 30 minutes .

B ① Could you take me to this address ?
② Could you take me to Tower Bridge ?
③ How long does it take to get to the airport ?
④ How long does it take to get to the beach ?

07 地下鐵 75 頁

A ① Do you know where the ticket office is?
② I need a one-day pass .
③ It's downstairs .

B ① Do you know where the elavator is?
② Do you know where the ticket machine is?
③ I need a one-way ticket .
④ I need a subway map .

08 入住飯店 85 頁

A ① I'd like to check in.
② What kind of room would you like?
③ I'd like a room with a single bed.

B ① I'd like to change my room .
② I'd like to order room service .
③ I'd like a room with a double bed .
④ I'd like a room with an ocean view .

使用飯店設施、服務

91 頁

A ① Where is the restaurant ?
② It's located on the third floor .
③ Is there room service?

B ① Where is the convenience store ?
② Where is the swimming pool ?
③ Is there free WiFi ?
④ Is there laundry service ?

解決飯店的問題

97 頁

A ① The air conditioner doesn't work .
② There is no toilet paper .
③ Oh, I'm sorry for any inconvenience.

B ① The telephone doesn't work.
② The heater doesn't work.
③ There is no towel .
④ There is no razor .

11 飯店退房

103 頁

A ① How would you like to pay ?
② Is it possible to pay by credit card?
③ I'm sorry for the error .

B ① I'm sorry for the delay .
② I'm sorry for calling so early .
③ Is it possible to check out late ?
④ Is it possible to leave my luggage here ?

12 預訂餐廳

113 頁

A ① I'd like to book a table for tonight.
② I'm sorry, but we are fully booked.
③ Could we have a table by the window ?

B ① I'd like to book a table for this Friday .
② I'd like to book a table for tomorrow night .
③ Could we have a table for two ?
④ Could we have a table in the corner ?

13 點餐

119 頁

A ① Does it come with a salad?
② What do you recommend for a main dish ?
③ The fish and chips are very good here.

B ① Does it come with bread ?
② Does it come with rice ?
③ What do you recommend for dessert ?
④ What do you recommend for dressing ?

對餐廳的不滿之處

125 頁

A ① This is too salty .
② I didn't order a salad .
③ I'll bring you what you ordered.

B ① I didn't order spaghetti .
② I didn't order ice cream .
③ This is too tough .
④ This is too cold .

速食餐廳

131 頁

A ① May I take your order ?
② I'd like a cheeseburger.
③ No ice , please.

B ① I'd like a hot dog .
② I'd like French fries .
③ No onions , please.
④ No ketchup , please.

16 咖啡廳

137 頁

A ① What can I get you?

② I'll have a latte.

③ Can you give me a sleeve ?

B ① I'll have an espresso .

② I'll have a cappuccino .

③ Can you give me a straw ?

④ Can you give me some sugar ?

17 買衣服

149 頁

A ① I'm looking for a jacket .

② Do you have this in a bigger size?

③ Here is a Large .

B ① I'm looking for a vest .

② I'm looking for jeans .

③ Do you have this in black .

④ Do you have this in a Medium .

18 殺價

155 頁

A ① How much is this watch ?

② It's 20 dollars .

③ Are these watches on sale ?

B ① How much is this tie ?
② How much are these shoes ?
③ Are these socks on sale?
④ Are these earrings on sale?

換貨與退貨

161 頁

A ① Can I exchange this for a bigger size?
② I'd like to get a refund on this skirt .
③ I'm sorry, but you can only exchange it.

B ① Can I exchange this for a different size ?
② Can I exchange this for a blue one ?
③ I'd like to get a refund on this hat .
④ I'd like to get a refund on these pants .

旅遊諮詢處

171 頁

A ① Can you recommend an interesting museum ?
② Are there any tours ?
③ Here are some brochures .

B ① Can you recommend a famous restaurant ?
② Can you recommend a nice hotel ?
③ Are there any local festivals ?
④ Are there any city tours ?

21 劇院

177 頁

A ① One ticket for Cats, please.
② What time does the show start ?
③ At 2 o'clock .

B ① One ticket for *Jekyll and Hyde* , please.
② One ticket for *The Lion King* , please.
③ What time does the musical start?
④ What time does the concert start?

22 博物館

183 頁

A ① What time does the museum close today?
② Where can I get a map of the museum?
③ You can get one at the front desk.

B ① What time does the art museum close today?
② What time does the zoo close today?
③ Where can I buy a ticket ?
④ Where can I get a brochure ?

23 找路

193 頁

A ① How can I get to Central Park?
② Where is the nearest bus stop?
③ Go straight and turn left at the corner .

B ① How can I get to the Korean embassy ?
② How can I get to Liberty Island ?
③ Where is the nearest department store ?
④ Where is the nearest subway station ?

失竊報案

199 頁

A ① Is there a police station around here?
② Yes. There's one across the street.
③ My bag was stolen .

B ① Is there a bank around here?
② Is there a hospital around here?
③ My wallet was stolen.
④ My cellphone was stolen.

登機手續

209 頁

A ① Can I have a window seat?
② I'm sorry, but they are all taken .
③ Can I see your passport ?

B ① Can I see your driver's license ?
② Can I see your boarding pass ?
③ Can I have an aisle seat ?
④ Can I have an exit-row seat ?

第三部分
認識更多

讓旅行變簡單的
句型造句練習

在這裡將前面所學過的句型和單字整合起來，並將「中文翻譯＋英文句子」一起錄音，以練習口說。請試著進行先聽中文，再說出英文的訓練。反覆聆聽並跟著唸的話，就能再國外旅遊時流暢地說出英語！

句型01 Would you like ________?

28 頁　請問你想要～嗎？

26-01

Would you like something to drink? 請問你要喝點什麼嗎？

Would you like chicken or beef? 請問你想要雞肉還是牛肉？

Would you like a glass of wine? 請問你想要一杯葡萄酒嗎？

Would you like some peanuts? 請問你想要一些花生嗎？

Would you like some water? 請問你想要一點水嗎？

句型02 ________, please.

29 頁　（請給我）～，謝謝。

26-02

Beef, **please.** （請給我）牛肉，謝謝。

Chicken, **please.** （請給我）雞肉，謝謝。

Fish, **please.** （請給我）魚，謝謝。

Orange juice, **please.** （請給我）柳橙汁，謝謝。

Coke, **please.** （請給我）可樂，謝謝。

Coffee, **please.** （請給我）咖啡，謝謝。

A beer, **please.** （請給我）一杯啤酒，謝謝。

句型03

Can I get ________?

34 頁　可以給我～嗎？

Can I get a blanket? 可以給我一條毯子嗎？

Can I get a newspaper? 可以給我一份報紙嗎？

Can I get a pen? 可以給我一枝筆嗎？

Can I get a pillow? 可以給我一個枕頭嗎？

Can I get a sleeping mask? 可以給我一副（睡眠用）眼罩嗎？

Can I get earplugs? 可以給我耳塞嗎？

Can I get headphones? 可以給我耳機嗎？

Could you ________?

35 頁　能請你～嗎？

Could you take my tray? 能請你收走我的托盤嗎？

Could you help me? 能請你幫忙我嗎？

Could you wake me for meals? 能請你在用餐時叫醒我嗎？

Could you move your seat up? 能請你豎直椅背嗎？

Could you switch seats with me? 能請你和我交換位子嗎？

句型05

I'm here ________.

44 頁

我來這裡～。

26-05

I'm here for sightseeing. 我來這裡觀光。

I'm here on vacation. 我來這裡度假。

I'm here on business. 我來這裡出差。

I'm here to visit my friend. 我來這裡拜訪朋友。

I'm here to study English. 我來這裡學英文。

句型06

I plan to stay for ________.

45 頁

我計畫待～。

26-06

I plan to stay for ten days. 我計畫待十天。

I plan to stay for three days. 我計畫待三天。

I plan to stay for a week. 我計畫待一週。

I plan to stay for two weeks. 我計畫待兩週。

I plan to stay for a month. 我計畫待一個月。

I plan to stay for two months. 我計畫待兩個月。

I plan to stay for about ten days. 我計畫待大約十天。

What's your ________?

50 頁 你的～是什麼？

26-07

What's your flight number? 你的航班號碼是什麼（幾號）？

What's your name? 你的姓名是什麼？

What's your home address? 你的住家地址是什麼？

What's your nationality? 你的國籍是什麼？

What's your phone number? 你的電話號碼是什麼（幾號）？

What's your seat number? 你的座位號碼是什麼（幾號）？

What's your final destination? 你的最終目的地是什麼（哪裡）？

Do you have ________?

51 頁 你有～嗎？

26-08

Do you have your baggage claim ticket? 你有行李託運存根嗎？

Do you have any liquids? 你有（任何）液體嗎？

Do you have any sharp objects? 你有（任何）尖銳物品嗎？

Do you have any carry-on bags? 你有（任何）手提行李嗎？

Do you have anything to declare? 你有（任何）須向海關申報的物品嗎？

句型09

Which bus goes to ________?

60 頁　哪班公車會到～？

26-09

Which bus goes to Times Square? 哪班公車會到時代廣場？

Which bus goes to the concert hall? 哪班公車會到演奏廳？

Which bus goes to the baseball stadium? 哪班公車會到棒球場？

Which bus goes to the British Museum? 哪班公車會到大英博物館？

Which bus goes to Victoria Station? 哪班公車會到維多利亞站？

句型10

Does this bus go to ________?

61 頁　這班公車會到～嗎？

26-10

Does this bus go to Times Square? 這班公車會到時代廣場嗎？

Does this bus go to Wall Street? 這班公車會到華爾街嗎？

Does this bus go to Fifth Avenue? 這班公車會到第五大道嗎？

Does this bus go to City Hall? 這班公車會到市政府嗎？

Does this bus go to Chicago? 這班公車會到芝加哥嗎？

Does this bus go to Manly Beach? 這班公車會到曼利海灘嗎？

Does this bus go to Chinatown? 這班公車會到中國城嗎？

Could you take me to ________?

66 頁

可以請你帶我去～嗎？

26-11

Could you take me to the Sun Hotel? 可以請你帶我去 Sun 飯店嗎？

Could you take me to this address? 可以請你帶我去這個地址嗎？

Could you take me to Sydney Tower? 可以請你帶我去雪梨塔嗎？

Could you take me to the GE Building? 可以請你帶我去 GE（奇異）大樓嗎？

Could you take me to Tower Bridge? 可以請你帶我去倫敦塔橋嗎？

How long does it take to get to ______?

67 頁

到～要花多久時間？

26-12

How long does it take to get to the hotel?
到飯店要花多久時間？

How long does it take to get to the airport?
到機場要花多久時間？

How long does it take to get to the bus station?
到巴士轉運站要花多久時間？

How long does it take to get to the university?
到大學要花多久時間？

How long does it take to get to the beach?
到海邊要花多久時間？

How long does it take to get to the mall?
到購物中心要花多久時間？

How long does it take to get to the city center?
到市中心要花多久時間？

句型 13

72 頁

Do you know where ________ is?

你知道～在哪裡嗎？

26-13

Do you know where the ticket office **is**?
你知道售票處在哪裡嗎？

Do you know where the ticket machine **is**?
你知道自動售票機在哪裡嗎？

Do you know where Platform 1 **is**?
你知道 1 號月台在哪裡嗎？

Do you know where the elevator **is**?
你知道電梯在哪裡嗎？

Do you know where the luggage locker area **is**?
你知道置物櫃區在哪裡嗎？

句型 14

73 頁

I need ________.

我需要～。

26-14

I need a one-day pass. 我需要一張一日票。

I need a one-way ticket. 我需要一張單程票。

I need a round-trip ticket. 我需要一張來回票。

I need a subway map. 我需要一張地下鐵地圖。

I need a MetroCard. 我需要一張 MetroCard。

I'd like to ________.

82 頁

我想要～。

26-15

I'd like to check in. 我想要辦理入住。

I'd like to order room service. 我想要叫客房服務。

I'd like to get laundry service. 我想要使用洗衣服務。

I'd like to change my room. 我想要換房間。

I'd like to make a reservation. 我想要預訂。

I'd like a room with ________.

83 頁

我想要一間有～的房間。

26-16

I'd like a room with a single bed. 我想要一間有一張單人床的房間。

I'd like a room with a double bed. 我想要一間有一張雙人床的房間。

I'd like a room with twin beds. 我想要一間有兩張單人床的房間。

I'd like a room with an ocean view. 我想要一間有海景的房間。

I'd like a room with a balcony. 我想要一間有陽台的房間。

句型17 Where is the ________?

88 頁

～在哪裡？

26-17

Where is the restaurant? 餐廳在哪裡？

Where is the front desk? 櫃台在哪裡？

Where is the lobby? 大廳在哪裡？

Where is the sauna? 桑拿室在哪裡？

Where is the fitness center? 健身中心在哪裡？

Where is the convenience store? 便利商店在哪裡？

Where is the swimming pool? 游泳池在哪裡？

句型18 Is there ________?

89 頁

有～嗎？

26-18

Is there room service? 有客房服務嗎？

Is there laundry service? 有洗衣服務嗎？

Is there valet parking? 有代客停車嗎？

Is there a wake-up call service? 有晨喚服務嗎？

Is there free WiFi? 有免費無線網路嗎？

The ______ doesn't work.

94 頁 ～故障了。

26-19

The air conditioner **doesn't work.** 空調故障了。

The heater **doesn't work.** 暖氣故障了。

The shower **doesn't work.** 淋浴間故障了。

The remote control **doesn't work.** 遙控器故障了。

The lamp **doesn't work.** 檯燈故障了。

The telephone **doesn't work.** 電話故障了。

The fridge **doesn't work.** 冰箱故障了。

There is no ________.

95 頁 沒有～。

26-20

There is no toilet paper. 沒有衛生紙。

There is no towel. 沒有毛巾。

There is no shampoo. 沒有洗髮乳。

There is no soap. 沒有肥皂。

There is no toothbrush. 沒有牙刷。

There is no hairdryer. 沒有吹風機。

There is no razor. 沒有刮鬍刀。

句型21 I'm sorry for ________.

100 頁

對於～，我很抱歉。

26-21

I'm sorry for the error. 對於這個錯誤，我很抱歉。

I'm sorry for the mistake. 對於這個失誤，我很抱歉。

I'm sorry for the delay. 對於這個延遲，我很抱歉。

I'm sorry for calling so early. 對於這麼早打電話來，我很抱歉。

I'm sorry for being late. 對於遲到，我很抱歉。

句型22 Is it possible to ________?

101 頁

可以～嗎？

26-22

Is it possible to pay by credit card?
可以用信用卡結帳嗎？

Is it possible to check out late?
可以晚點退房嗎？

Is it possible to leave my luggage here?
可以把我的行李寄放在這裡嗎？

Is it possible to stay one more night?
可以多住一晚嗎？

Is it possible to leave a day earlier?
可以早一天離開嗎？

I'd like to book a table for ________.

110 頁　我想預訂～的位子。

26-23

I'd like to book a table for tonight. 我想預訂今天晚上的位子。

I'd like to book a table for 11 a.m. 我想預訂上午 11 點的位子。

I'd like to book a table for 7 p.m. 我想預訂晚上 7 點的位子。

I'd like to book a table for 6 o'clock. 我想預訂 6 點整的位子。

I'd like to book a table for tomorrow night. 我想預訂明天晚上的位子。

I'd like to book a table for Sunday lunch. 我想預訂星期日午餐的位子。

I'd like to book a table for this Friday. 我想預訂這個星期五的位子。

Could we have a table ________?

111 頁　我們可以坐～的座位嗎？

26-24

Could we have a table by the window?
我們可以坐窗邊的座位嗎？

Could we have a table for two?
我們可以坐兩人座的座位嗎？

Could we have a table on the terrace?
我們可以坐在露臺的座位嗎？

Could we have a table in the non-smoking area?
我們可以坐在禁菸區的座位嗎？

Could we have a table in the corner?
我們可以坐在角落的座位嗎？

句型 25

Does it come with ________?

116 頁　這個有附～嗎？

26-25

Does it come with a salad? 這個有附沙拉嗎？

Does it come with a drink? 這個有附飲料嗎？

Does it come with rice? 這個有附白飯嗎？

Does it come with soup? 這個有附湯嗎？

Does it come with bread? 這個有附麵包嗎？

Does it come with pickles? 這個有附醃黃瓜嗎？

Does it come with vegetables? 這個有附蔬菜嗎？

句型 26

What do you recommend for ________?

117 頁　你推薦什麼作為～？

26-26

What do you recommend for a main dish? 你推薦什麼作為主餐？

What do you recommend for an appetizer? 你推薦什麼作為前菜？

What do you recommend for a side dish? 你推薦什麼作為附餐？

What do you recommend for dessert? 你推薦什麼作為甜點？

What do you recommend for dressing? 你推薦什麼作為醬汁（哪種醬汁）？

What do you recommend for wine? 你推薦什麼作為葡萄酒（哪種酒）？

What do you recommend for a fish dish? 你推薦什麼作為魚肉料理（哪道魚肉料理）？

This is too ________.

122 頁　這個太～了。

26-27

This is too salty. 這個太鹹了。

This is too spicy. 這個太辣了。

This is too sour. 這個太酸了。

This is too cold. 這個太涼了。

This is too tough. 這個（肉）太韌了。

This is too pink. 這個（肉）太生了。

This is too bitter. 這個太苦了。

I didn't order ________.

123 頁　我沒有點～。

26-28

I didn't order a salad. 我沒有點沙拉。

I didn't order spaghetti. 我沒有點義大利麵。

I didn't order tomato soup. 我沒有點番茄湯。

I didn't order a steak. 我沒有點牛排。

I didn't order roast beef. 我沒有點烤牛肉。

I didn't order ice cream. 我沒有點冰淇淋。

I didn't order a stew. 我沒有點燉菜。

句型29 128 頁

I'd like ________.

我要～。

I'd like a cheeseburger. 我要一個起司漢堡。

I'd like a number 3. 我要一個 3 號餐。

I'd like a chicken burger. 我要一個雞肉漢堡。

I'd like a hot dog. 我要一個熱狗。

I'd like a Whopper. 我要一個華堡。

I'd like French fries. 我要炸薯條。

I'd like a biscuit. 我要一個比司吉。

26-29

句型30 129 頁

No ________, please.

不要／去掉～，**謝謝**。

No ice, **please**. 不要冰塊，謝謝。

No ketchup, **please**. 不要番茄醬，謝謝。

No mayo, **please**. 不要美乃滋，謝謝。

No syrup, **please**. 不要糖漿，謝謝。

No whipped cream, **please**. 不要鮮奶油，謝謝。

No onions, **please**. 不要洋蔥，謝謝。

No cucumber, **please**. 不要黃瓜，謝謝。

26-30

I'll have ________.

134 頁 我要~。

26-31

I'll have a latte. 我要一杯拿鐵。

I'll have an espresso. 我要一杯義式濃縮咖啡。

I'll have an Americano. 我要一杯美式咖啡。

I'll have a cappuccino. 我要一杯卡布奇諾。

I'll have a cafe mocha. 我要一杯摩卡咖啡。

I'll have an iced tea. 我要一杯冰茶。

I'll have a hot chocolate. 我要一杯熱巧克力。

Can you give me ________?

135 頁 你可以給我~嗎？

26-32

Can you give me a sleeve? 你可以給我一個杯套嗎？

Can you give me a straw? 你可以給我一根吸管嗎？

Can you give me a fork? 你可以給我一支叉子嗎？

Can you give me a lid? 你可以給我一個杯蓋嗎？

Can you give me a receipt? 你可以給我收據嗎？

Can you give me some napkins? 你可以給我一些餐巾紙嗎？

Can you give me some sugar? 你可以給我一些糖嗎？

句型33 I'm looking for ________.

146 頁 我正在找～。

26-33

I'm looking for a jacket. 我正在找一件夾克。

I'm looking for a shirt. 我正在找一件襯衫。

I'm looking for a blouse. 我正在找一件女用襯衫。

I'm looking for a vest. 我正在找一件背心。

I'm looking for a coat. 我正在找一件大衣。

I'm looking for jeans. 我正在找牛仔褲。

I'm looking for shorts. 我正在找短褲。

句型34 Do you have this in ________?

147 頁 （你們）這個有～的嗎？

26-34

Do you have this in a bigger size? （你們）這個有更大的尺寸嗎？

Do you have this in a Medium? （你們）這個有 M 號的嗎？

Do you have this in a size 8? （你們）這個有 8 號的嗎？

Do you have this in a smaller size? （你們）這個有更小號的嗎？

Do you have this in red? （你們）這個有紅色的嗎？

Do you have this in black? （你們）這個有黑色的嗎？

Do you have this in beige? （你們）這個有米色的嗎？

How much is [are] ________?

152 頁 ～多少錢？

26-35

How much is this watch? 這隻手錶多少錢？

How much is this tie? 這條領帶多少錢？

How much is this lipstick? 這支唇膏多少錢？

How much is this perfume? 這瓶香水多少錢？

How much are these shoes? 這雙鞋多少錢？

How much are these gloves? 這雙手套多少錢？

How much are these sunglasses? 這副太陽眼鏡多少錢？

Are these ________ on sale?

153 頁 這些～在特價嗎？

26-36

Are these watches **on sale**? 這些手錶在特價嗎？

Are these T-shirts **on sale**? 這些 T 恤在特價嗎？

Are these suits **on sale**? 這些西裝在特價嗎？

Are these earrings **on sale**? 這些耳環在特價嗎？

Are these caps **on sale**? 這些鴨舌帽在特價嗎？

Are these belts **on sale**? 這些皮帶在特價嗎？

Are these socks **on sale**? 這些襪子在特價嗎？

句型37

158 頁

Can I exchange this for ________?

我可以把這個可以換成～嗎？

26-37

Can I exchange this for a bigger size?
我可以把這個換成更大的尺寸嗎？

Can I exchange this for a different size?
我可以把這個換成其他尺寸嗎？

Can I exchange this for a different color?
我可以把這個換成其他顏色嗎？

Can I exchange this for a blue one?
我可以把這個換成藍色的嗎？

Can I exchange this for a white one?
我可以把這個換成白色的嗎？

句型38

159 頁

I'd like to get a refund on ________.

我想退～。

26-38

I'd like to get a refund on this skirt. 我想退這件裙子。

I'd like to get a refund on this scarf. 我想退這條圍巾。

I'd like to get a refund on this dress. 我想退這件洋裝。

I'd like to get a refund on this hat. 我想退這頂帽子。

I'd like to get a refund on these pajamas. 我想退這套睡衣。

I'd like to get a refund on these pants. 我想退這條褲子。

I'd like to get a refund on these sandals. 我想退這雙涼鞋。

Can you recommend ________?

168 頁 你可以推薦～嗎？

26-39

Can you recommend an interesting museum?
你可以推薦有趣的博物館嗎？

Can you recommend a good musical?
你可以推薦不錯的音樂劇嗎？

Can you recommend a famous restaurant?
你可以推薦有名的餐廳嗎？

Can you recommend some tourist attractions?
你可以推薦一些觀光景點嗎？

Can you recommend a nice hotel?
你可以推薦好的飯店嗎？

Are there any ________?

169 頁 有（任何）～嗎？

26-40

Are there any tours? 有（任何）遊覽行程嗎？

Are there any city tours? 有（任何）城市遊覽行程嗎？

Are there any night tours? 有（任何）夜間遊覽行程嗎？

Are there any sporting events? 有（任何）運動賽事嗎？

Are there any local festivals? 有（任何）地方節慶嗎？

句型41

One ticket for ________, please.

174 頁　（請給我）一張～的票，謝謝。

26-41

One ticket for *Cats*, **please.**
（請給我）一張《貓》的票，謝謝。

One ticket for *The Lion King*, **please.**
（請給我）一張《獅子王》的票，謝謝。

One ticket for *Jekyll and Hyde*, **please.**
（請給我）一張《變身怪醫》的票，謝謝。

One ticket for *Les Miserables*, **please.**
（請給我）一張《悲慘世界》的票，謝謝。

One ticket for *The Phantom of the Opera*, **please.**
（請給我）一張《歌劇魅影》的票，謝謝。

句型42

What time does the ________ start?

175 頁　～幾點開始？

26-42

What time does the show **start?** 表演幾點開始？

What time does the movie **start?** 電影幾點開始？

What time does the opera **start?** 歌劇幾點開始？

What time does the musical **start?** 音樂劇幾點開始？

What time does the play **start?** 舞台劇幾點開始？

What time does the ballet **start?** 芭蕾舞幾點開始？

What time does the concert **start?** 音樂會幾點開始？

What time does the _____ close today?

180 頁 今天～幾點關閉？

26-43

What time does the museum **close today**?
今天博物館幾點關閉？

What time does the palace **close today**?
今天宮殿幾點關閉？

What time does the zoo **close today**?
今天動物園幾點關閉？

What time does the aquarium **close today**?
今天水族館幾點關閉？

What time does the cathedral **close today**?
今天大教堂幾點關閉？

What time does the art museum **close today**?
今天美術館幾點關閉？

What time does the botanical garden **close today**?
今天植物園幾點關閉？

Where can I _________?

181 頁 我可以在哪裡～？

26-44

Where can I get a map of the museum? 我可以在哪裡拿到博物館地圖？

Where can I buy a ticket? 我可以在哪裡買票？

Where can I find the restroom? 我可以在哪裡找到廁所？

Where can I rent an audio guide? 我可以在哪裡租借語音導覽？

Where can I get a brochure? 我可以在哪裡拿到介紹手冊？

句型45 How can I get to ________?

190 頁　我要怎麼去～？

26-45

How can I get to Central Park?
我要怎麼去中央公園？

How can I get to the Korean embassy?
我要怎麼去韓國大使館？

How can I get to the natural history museum?
我要怎麼去自然史博物館？

How can I get to Liberty Island?
我要怎麼去自由島？

How can I get to Queen's Theater?
我要怎麼去皇后劇院？

句型46 Where is the nearest ________?

191 頁　最近的～在哪裡？

26-46

Where is the nearest bus stop?　最近的公車站牌在哪裡？

Where is the nearest taxi stand?　最近的計程車招呼站在哪裡？

Where is the nearest subway station?　最近的地鐵站在哪裡？

Where is the nearest department store?　最近的百貨公司在哪裡？

Where is the nearest supermarket?　最近的超級市場在哪裡？

句型47

Is there a [an] ________ around here?

196 頁　這附近有～嗎？

26-47

Is there a police station **around here**? 這附近有警察局嗎？

Is there a hospital **around here**? 這附近有醫院嗎？

Is there a drugstore **around here**? 這附近有藥妝店嗎？

Is there a restroom **around here**? 這附近有洗手間嗎？

Is there a bank **around here**? 這附近有銀行嗎？

Is there a post office **around here**? 這附近有郵局嗎？

Is there a pay phone **around here**? 這附近有公共電話嗎？

句型48

My ________ was stolen.

197 頁　我的～被偷了。

26-48

My bag **was stolen**. 我的包包被偷了。

My wallet **was stolen**. 我的皮夾被偷了。

My backpack **was stolen**. 我的背包被偷了。

My handbag **was stolen**. 我的手提包被偷了。

My cellphone **was stolen**. 我的手機被偷了。

My credit card **was stolen**. 我的信用卡被偷了。

My camera **was stolen**. 我的相機被偷了。

句型49 Can I see your ________?

206 頁

我可以看看你的～嗎？

26-49

Can I see your passport? 我可以看看你的護照嗎？

Can I see your boarding pass? 我可以看看你的登機證嗎？

Can I see your customs form? 我可以看看你的關稅申報單嗎？

Can I see your driver's license? 我可以看看你的駕照嗎？

Can I see your ticket? 我可以看看你的票嗎？

句型50 Can I have ________?

207 頁

我可以坐～嗎？

26-50

Can I have a window seat? 我可以坐靠窗的座位嗎？

Can I have an aisle seat? 我可以坐靠走道的座位嗎？

Can I have an exit-row seat? 我可以坐緊急逃生口旁的座位嗎？

Can I have a first-row seat? 我可以坐最前排的座位嗎？

Can I have a seat next to my friend? 我可以坐我朋友旁邊的座位嗎？

互有不同的
美式英語
vs.
英式英語

英語是美國、英國、澳洲、紐西蘭等許多國家的主要語言。不過，在不同國家，也會使用不同的單字來表達相同意思。讓我們來認識美式英語和英式英語中，同義不同用字最具代表性的例子。

場所

27-1

movie theater [ˋmuvɪ ˋθɪətɚ]	電影院	**cinema** [ˋsɪnəmə]
gas station [gæs ˋsteʃən]	加油站	**petrol station** [ˋpɛtrəl ˋsteʃən]
parking lot [ˋparkɪŋ lɑt]	停車場	**car park** [kɑr park]
first floor [fɝst flor]	一樓	**ground floor** [graʊnd flor]
second floor [ˋsɛkənd flor]	二樓	**first floor** [fɝst flor]
front desk [frʌnt dɛsk]	前台	**reception** [rɪˋsɛpʃən]
elevator [ˋɛlə͵vetɚ]	電梯	**lift** [lɪft]
restroom [ˋrɛst͵rum]	洗手間	**toilet** [ˋtɔɪlɪt]

27-2

(French) fries [(frɛntʃ) fraɪz]	炸薯條	**chips** [tʃɪps]
(potato) chips [(pə`teto) tʃɪps]	洋芋片	**crisps** [krɪsps]
shrimp [ʃrɪmp]	蝦子	**prawn** [prɔn]
cookie [`kʊkɪ]	餅乾	**biscuit** [`bɪskɪt]
candy [`kændɪ]	甜食	**sweet** [swit]
corn [kɔrn]	玉米	**maize** [mez]
powdered sugar [`paʊdɚd `ʃʊgɚ]	糖粉	**icing sugar** [`aɪsɪŋ `ʃʊgɚ]
appetizer [`æpə͵taɪzɚ]	前菜	**starter** [`stɑrtɚ]

27-3

subway [ˋsʌbˏwe]	**地下鐵**	**underground** [ˋʌndɚˏgraʊnd]
bus [bʌs]	**長途巴士**	**coach** [kotʃ]
one-way ticket [ˋwʌnˏwe ˋtɪkɪt]	**單程票**	**single ticket** [ˋsɪŋgəl ˋtɪkɪt]
round-trip ticket [ˋraʊndˏtrɪp ˋtɪkɪt]	**來回票**	**return ticket** [rɪˋtɝn ˋtɪkɪt]
freeway [ˋfrɪˏwe]	**高速公路**	**motorway** [ˋmotɚˏwe]
railroad [ˋrelˏrod]	**鐵路**	**railway** [ˋrelˏwe]
sidewalk [ˋsaɪdˏwɔk]	**人行道**	**pavement** [ˋpevmənt]
crosswalk [ˋkrɔsˏwɔk]	**行人穿越道**	**pedestrian crossing** [pəˋdɛstrɪən ˋkrɔsɪŋ]

27-4

pants [pænts]	褲子	**trousers** [`traʊzɚz]
sweater [`swɛtɚ]	毛衣	**jumper** [`dʒʌmpɚ]
sneakers [`snikɚz]	運動鞋	**trainers** [`trenɚz]
undershirt [`ʌndɚ͵ʃɝt]	汗衫、內衣	**vest** [vɛst]
vest [vɛst]	（男用）背心	**waistcoat** [`west͵kot]
underpants [`ʌndɚ͵pænts]	內褲	**pants** [pænts]
turtleneck [`tɝt!͵nɛk]	高領毛衣 （或指高領毛衣的領子）	**polo neck** [`polo nɛk]
zipper [`zɪpɚ]	拉鍊	**zip** [zɪp]

27-5

closet [ˋklɑzɪt]	衣櫃	**wardrobe** [ˋwɔrd͵rob]
trash can [træʃ kæn]	垃圾桶	**dustbin** [ˋdʌst͵bɪn]
bathtub [ˋbæθ͵tʌb]	浴缸	**bath** [bæθ]
gas stove [gæs stov]	瓦斯爐	**gas cooker** [gæs ˋkʊkɚ]
cellphone [ˋsɛlfon]	手機	**mobile (phone)** [ˋmobɪl (fon)]
flashlight [ˋflæʃ͵laɪt]	手電筒	**torch** [tɔrtʃ]
Band-Aid [ˋbænd͵ed]	OK 繃	**plaster** [ˋpletɚ]
can [kæn]	罐頭	**tin** [tɪn]

vacation [veˋkeʃən]	假日、休假	**holiday** [ˋhɑlə͵de]
public holiday [ˋpʌblɪk ˋhɑlə͵de]	國定假日	**bank holiday** [bæŋk ˋhɑlə͵de]
soccer [ˋsɑkɚ]	足球	**football** [ˋfʊt͵bɔl]
football [ˋfʊt͵bɔl]	美式足球	**American football** [əˋmɛrɪkən ˋfʊt͵bɔl]
zip code [zɪp kod]	郵遞區號	**postcode** [ˋpost͵kod]
fall [fɔl]	秋天	**autumn** [ˋɔtəm]
check [tʃɛk]	帳單	**bill** [bɪl]
takeout [ˋtek͵aʊt]	外帶	**takeaway** [ˋtekə͵we]

拼法不同的單字

27-7

color [`kʌlɚ]	顏色	**colour** [`kʌlɚ]
theater [`θɪətɚ]	劇院	**theatre** [`θɪətɚ]
center [`sɛntɚ]	中心	**centre** [`sɛntɚ]
traveler [`trævəlɚ]	旅行者	**traveller** [`trævəlɚ]
check [tʃɛk]	支票	**cheque** [tʃɛk]
jewelry [`dʒuəlrɪ]	珠寶	**jewellery** [`dʒuəlrɪ]
pajamas [pə`dʒæməs]	睡衣	**pyjamas** [pə`dʒæməs]
whiskey [`hwɪskɪ]	威士忌	**whisky** [`hwɪskɪ]

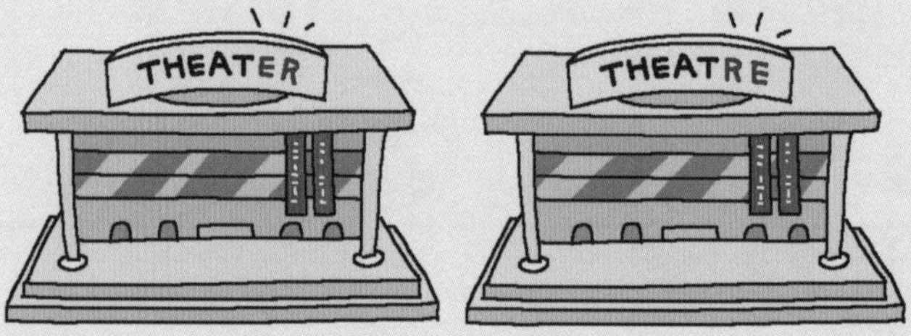

辛苦了^^

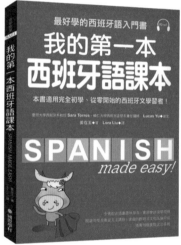

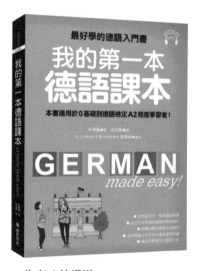

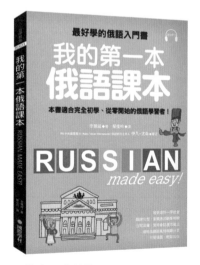

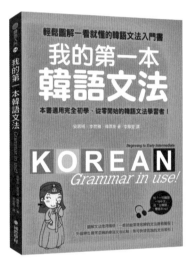

台灣廣廈 國際出版集團
Taiwan Mansion International Group

國家圖書館出版品預行編目（CIP）資料

我的第一本中高齡旅遊英語：簡簡單單一句就搞定！跟團、自由行、自學教學都好用！/ 裴鎮英，姜旼正 著.
-- 新北市：國際學村，2019.1
面；　公分.
ISBN 978-986-454-094-5(平裝附光碟片)

1. 英語 2. 旅遊 3. 會話

805.188　　107017824

國際學村

我的第一本中高齡旅遊英語

簡簡單單一句就搞定！跟團、自由行、自學教學都好用！

作　　者／裴鎮英、姜旼正
譯　　者／胡至葦
編輯中心／第七編輯室
編 輯 長／伍峻宏・**編輯**／鄭琦諭
封面設計／林嘉瑜・**內頁排版**／菩薩蠻數位文化有限公司
製版・印刷・裝訂／東豪／弼聖／明和

發 行 人／江媛珍
法律顧問／第一國際法律事務所 余淑杏律師・北辰著作權事務所 蕭雄淋律師
出　　版／台灣廣廈有聲圖書有限公司
地址：新北市235中和區中山路二段359巷7號2樓
電話：（886）2-2225-5777・傳真：（886）2-2225-8052

行企研發中心總監／陳冠蒨
整合行銷組／陳宜鈴
媒體公關組／徐毓庭
綜合業務組／何欣穎
地址：新北市234永和區中和路345號18樓之2
電話：（886）2-2922-8181・傳真：（886）2-2929-5132

代理印務・全球總經銷／知遠文化事業有限公司
地址：新北市222深坑區北深路三段155巷25號5樓
電話：（886）2-2664-8800・傳真：（886）2-2664-8801
郵 政 劃 撥／劃撥帳號：18836722
劃撥戶名：知遠文化事業有限公司（※單次購書金額未達1000元，請另付70元郵資。）

■出版日期：2018年12月初版
2024年07月7刷
ISBN：978-986-454-094-5